STILL LIFE
WITH
INSECTS

STILL LIFE
WITH
INSECTS

BRIAN
KITELEY

Ticknor & Fields
NEW YORK
1989

Library of Congress Cataloging-in-Publication Data

Kiteley, Brian.
Still life with insects / Brian Kiteley.
p.   cm.
ISBN 0-89919-898-8
I. Title.
PS3561.I855S75   1989
813'.54—dc19   88-35329
CIP

Printed in the United States of America

D   10   9   8   7   6   5   4   3   2   1

TO ERIC JAMES KITELEY

The world is never the less beautifull
though viewed through a chink or knot-hole.

THOREAU

STILL LIFE
WITH
INSECTS

man they fired when the boss discovered his M.A. still pops up in my wife's late-night chatter; I should never have told her. To come upon Drumheller the way I did reminded me of the feeling just before my breakdown: I knew what was coming, but still I was surprised. At the grain auction the boys from soil research wore party hats to celebrate my forty-third birthday and return to work. The candle I was supposed to blow out would not stand upright in the fist-sized flour dough effigy of the big boss. I said you can't hold a candle to him and everyone repeated this all day long. A little secretively I stopped at the dry riverbed outside of town and used my wife's empty Dramamine container as a holding bottle. Kirby's Backswimmer—or rather *Notonecta kirbyi*—never seems to touch the water. Under water, it can stop still for hours at any depth, patiently awaiting gnats and flies that land on the surface. I imitated its above-water stance: knees in the mud, bottom in the air, hands hugging earth, my eyes almost level with the filmy pool. But four teenagers in a farmer's truck hooted, "Going for a swim, old man?" The hollow ground echoed the approach of a freight train, like a thundering herd of the dinosaurs paleontologists keep discovering to the north. I nearly left the bottle behind but remembered we'd need the prescription sticker for a refill. A small sandstorm blew up on my way to the car. Until I returned to the plateau and hill on the granite outface, the first ripple of the continental shield that extends a thousand miles into Canada. I asked what this voice said. "Don't laugh," she said. " 'Bury me.' I think it was a ghost—very soft, maybe dead a long time." I had to chuckle. In the pit of an outhouse? What a fate. "Listen," she commanded. The trees of the taller inland forest groaned. The lake sucked the sandy shore near us and slapped granite farther up. "I can't hear anything," I said. She told me to go inside. "Is this a trick?" I asked. "A surprise party maybe?" She breathed my name, as if blowing out candles. I entered and sat on the wooden seat and shined the light around the corners of the small room I had not yet seen in daylight. One corner had rotted through, I could tell by the change in the wood surface, to a dried-mud look. I heard a sharp clicking and my light caught the flash of silver. "Is that your ghost?" I asked. She leaned in the doorway. I shined the light off one of the pink walls so that her face was gently illuminated. "Yes." "It's only a beetle," I whispered. "Land sakes," she said, "what else was I expecting?" I asked her to hold the flashlight. The clicking sounded like a Metallic Wood Borer. "No, come away from there. You'll catch a chill." But it was a warm night and she trained the light expertly on the rotted wood corner of the floor anyway. I had a small pair of tweezers in my pocket to dig with. My wife talked while I hunted. "I wish you'd speak with Henry about that girl he's seeing. You know she's twenty-five? That's six years older than him. He's so impressed with himself now, driving that cab. He thinks he can support her and go to college at the same time. I don't want him to make the same mistake you made." I looked up into the flashlight beam, curious. "What, marrying you?" I asked. "Go away," she said. "Henry's too independent. All that vagabonding on the railroads when he was younger. I know she's a nurse and in many respects a lovely young lady, but I can't see what she sees in him. He's still a baby. If you talked to him he'd listen, but you and he have barely said a word since your last episode." Two years ago my son had said he never wanted to talk to me again, when I was found wandering the stockyards in my pajamas. "Look," I said to my wife, displaying the two beetles, who were mating. "If you could see these lovers under a microscope you'd notice the male's terrifically barbed genital organ. I can't imagine how they separate after copulation." "Oh Elwyn!" she shrieked. "Put them down." She thrust the flashlight at me, but I let it fall. My hands were full, opening the killing bottle with one hand and holding the beetles in the other. The flashlight rolled on the ground and cast a long, snaking shadow off my wife as she retreated. Then she stood in the doorway of the cabin and waved, a strangely seductive combination of fear and authority. "You come back here this moment," she shouted. I remembered the honeymoon. A bat had flown into our room from the fireplace, and I, naked as I'd ever been, stood on the bed trying to sweep it out an open window with a broom. My wife had been terrified a moment earlier, but from underneath me she commanded, "Put down that weapon. He'll find his own way out."

Sifted out of wheat taken from corners and behind liners of empty boxcars. New Prague, Minnesota. July 22, 1950.

For a moment Robin Hood Flour sacks stacked high on a flatcar caught the setting sun. The notch created by the sack I ordered taken down to be checked for seed beetle infestation was a perfect fit for the flattened sun. I had the railroad yard employees move the whole load to a boxcar because of the threat of rain. This was not my job, but I saved them some trouble. They were grateful I pointed out the precaution, despite working so late, despite the cloudless skies. The old foreman believed my forecast without a wink. I stayed in the yard in the dark after they left, checking under rocks and around the cars. A pale aurora borealis swirled over the telephone wires and grain elevators to the north. My FDA agent startled me where I'd made a find. "I heard you were still out here ordering the boys around," he said as we sat down on the lip of the boxcar door. He was the reason I had come down to New Prague—a spot inspection of a shipment of our wheat. "I don't mind you doing my job," he said. "But I thought I'd make sure you weren't poaching on my territory. And look what I find." He held up my killing bottle, laughing. We shared the same peculiar hobby. We were planning a collecting trip to the Mississippi marshes near Winona the next day, if the weather held dry. "What you got? Don't tell me. Even in this light I can tell—*Cicindela lepida*. The Dainty Tiger Beetle. I see a few up on Superior and Huron, but you know they're rare for these parts—chiefly eastern shore beetles. What's this devil doing so far from home?" I asked him how he could tell what it was in the dark. "Elementary—the sparkling green prothorax, the hoary white underbelly, the fantail feelers, those distinctive checkered markings. You got to have good eyes to collect these buggers—buggers!" He rumbled like a small tractor. "Good ears, too. I overheard you talking to yourself about your catch. You ought to be a bit more secretive, man. You never know who's lurking about these yards." He sat in silence for a while as I packed my gear. The air was still and noisy. The tracks parallel to us reflected a far-off light, from a street lamp maybe, but not an approaching locomotive; the light did not waver. I mentioned the new FDA regulations, and my agent sighed. "If you ask me, we were getting more nutritious flour when all those beetle parts were ground into it. You and I know how much protein there is in a harmless hundred thousand small-eyed flour beetles." I said I had those regulations to thank for my new position in the company—chief of extermination research. Finally my half education was no longer a hindrance. "But think of your poor wife up there in Canader," my FDA agent said. "Selling a house. Packing up two kids. Moving to a new country. You're a cruel man." The new job also meant a transfer from Calgary to Minneapolis. "It's a cruel company," I said. "They told me to butter you up, but in good conscience I couldn't." "Good conscience!" he roared, slapping me on the back. "When shall we meet tomorrow?" I asked.

Sifted from Ontario soft winter wheat—under boxcar. Tuscaloosa, Alabama. April 2, 1951.

A luxury after thirteen towns in a week: two nights in the same place. Another buyer here tomorrow, Monday. Today: church, rest, the relatively easy naval supply base chief petty officer. "Shore am glad you all could come here on the Sabbath. Which religious leaning you have, sirs?" The traveling salesman from Robin Hood I hooked up with in New Orleans said, "Poker." "I've never played cards myself," the chief petty officer said, and from that point on he never spoke a word directly to the salesman.

I lay down on the track and the supply officer towered overhead. The earth smelled of rust, the salesman of tobacco juice, which he spit dangerously near to me. The chief petty officer tended to shift from one foot to another, rustling the heavy fabric of his trousers, which must have been devilish in this Alabama heat. My salesman stood completely still. He claimed the best way to keep his clients' attention was by gesture, constant movement of the hands and shoulders and head. But apparently his natural state was stillness. His preferred posture was this calm, oblique slouch. He was not on duty now. The naval supply base was an easy customer, fat money, and besides had already filled a year's order. I was the one on duty. I stared under the boxcar. The chief petty officer was worried some grain had escaped through holes in the floors, which made no difference to me. I was looking for a stray bag of flour with green mold, marked 0-19A. In Minneapolis it had been decided I would not tell anyone what I was really looking for. (The tainted flour had been discovered by accident and the company didn't want to alarm any customers.) I would simply say I was there to recommend proper hygiene procedures for storage and transport of flour. The tedious search for the 0–18 and 0–19 series, throughout Alabama, Mississippi, and Georgia, had to be relieved along the way by my own private search. Here, for the Striped Blister Beetle. But the salesman and the supply officer had no idea what I was doing.

"Shore is hot for April," the salesman said. Voice tight from being mimicked, the chief petty officer asked me, "Do you suspect the loading dock mayn't be another spot?" "Who the hell knows what this old coot's up to." My salesman winked at me when he said this. Standing, I handed him the blister beetle so that I could rummage through my bag.

"What the hell are you—" he said, but made a fist around the beetle anyway. He asked about the killing bottle, which I was opening. I explained its use, then told the salesman he might want to wash his hands. These beetles secrete a chemical, cantharidin, which blisters most human skin. "I am sorry," the supply officer said. "Water main repair this morning. The whole base been turned off. But the bay's only half a mile over yonder." I asked to see bag 0–19A, if it hadn't been opened. The chief petty officer, escorting me toward a building the size of an airplane hangar, asked if this blister beetle was one of the causes of "our poor hygiene." For a moment I felt a surge of guilt, deceiving this open-faced man about a possibly dangerous contamination of his supplies. But my salesman shouted, "Hey wait a minute," staring into his palm. "What about *your* hands? Why don't you get blisters?"

Over my shoulder I said, "I seem to be immune."

Large numbers in flight over open fields.
Twenty miles west of Saskatoon, near Biggar.
September 20, 1951.

The beetles I caught today had lost their way. Several hundred Cow Dung Beetles in flight. Miles and miles of food, but not the sort they can digest. They see—or smell—a forest of grain that should be the ideal grazing land for buffalo or cattle. Flying west was the right idea, but they are still a hundred miles from the cattle ranches of Alberta they want. I stood in several acres of our new hybrid wheat, which fights off the five major rusts and molds. People in the industry say it will be the only wheat grown in ten years. The utter simplicity of vegetation begs for a simplicity of pest. With only one food for miles around—and only one strain of that food—other insects find a terrifying abundance. Their instincts tell them to

eat what stimulates their simple olfactory nerves—
most insects can smell only a handful of odors. A
certain male moth smells nothing but the pheromone
of his mate, but he can detect that pheromone five
miles away. In a dozen square miles of wheat, the
pests are unable to stop eating. They reproduce insanely to meet the demand. I suggested mixing up the
breeds of wheat or growing legumes—using the old
rules of crop rotation—to keep the threat of pests
down. One fellow in yield research laughed. "You're
actually trying to outwit insects? Just spray them
dead." In British Columbia, where orchards are still
small businesses, farmers do use their wits. The de-
structive Coddling Moth lays her eggs only at twilight. A man I know said he hooked up floodlights
along the orchard rows and turned them on just before twilight. The confused moths waited. When to-
tal darkness fell, the farmer turned the lights off, and
the moths flew off without laying one egg in his
apples. When I described this to a vice-president, he
said, "You tell a great story, Farmer. I don't see what
it has to do with our business, but I'll keep you in
mind for presentations."

Drilling into exposed heartwood of a standing maple. Part of the tree had fallen, splitting a section of the trunk. Northfield, Minnesota. May 4, 1952.

The cook walked a wide arc around the empty dining room in the La Crosse Hotel and finally stopped at my table as if by accident. From his side appeared the bag lunch I'd ordered with my breakfast. This boy looked intelligent and too young to be a fry cook. He asked me what I was reading. "Just an entomology journal," I said, my gaze distracted by the dust motes and sunlight. Shadows of people too brightly lit to make out passed by the picture window on the street below. "Oh," he said, disappointed. "I want to write a novel. My dad wants me to go to work in his brother's bank." This comment hung in the air for a moment until I decided to clean my glasses with the cloth napkin. A middle-aged man entered from Division Street, bringing a gust of hot air. He carried a doctor's bag and frowned at me. "If you don't mind, sir," he said, "I'd like to have a word alone with my son." I never saw either of them again, but the way the father took his son by the neck, as if the boy were still a child, and his tone of voice with me, as if I were giving his son bad advice, reminded me of someone I could not quite place. The sandwiches the cook prepared, however, were excellent—Wisconsin cheddar so sharp my lips burned, oily ham, and great watery slices of tomato someone must have been sorely tempted to pick weeks before they finally arrived in my sandwiches.

After my appointment in La Crosse, I drove seventy miles before I stopped for lunch and a bit of collecting in a handsome wooded valley that lay between rolls of black farmland. An undergraduate field biology class came upon me—the forest belonged to their nearby college—and the professor asked me to talk about the sorts of insects I found in these parts. My little lecture and, later, the warm colors inside a stand of blooming red-osier dogwoods convinced me there was no need to rush off to Le Sueur, which was next on my itinerary. I had parked my car beside a phone booth crowded by these dogwoods. Inhaling the steamy smell of honey and burnt rope, I began to search the flowers for sap-drinking beetles. The telephone rang. I reached through branches and brambles into the phone booth, as if this were a perfectly natural thing to do.

"Hello?" I said.

"Dad," my son Henry said breathlessly. "I called Helen down at the central exchange and I asked if she could pretty please find the phone number of your field office—"

"Field office," I repeated, laughing. I had called my wife from this phone half an hour before to tell her I would not be home today after all.

Henry kept bantering along in the happy, excited

voice I had not heard since he and Helen broke off their engagement.

He was saying, "I told Helen it was a family emergency. I come home from a big philo exam and find a mother and baby brother looking about as glum as a couple of Ukrainians. I figured it would be easy to trace the call, since you called collect. In case you're wondering, the cost of this conversation is on Minnesota Bell, the monopoly with a heart."

Most people enjoy my son's sense of humor and storytelling, but no one as much as he does. He took a breath, and laughter strangled his efforts to refill his lungs.

"Dad," he said after a moment, "are you there?"

I nodded, watching a chipmunk on the bridle path through the phosphorescent green of early spring leaves. The path sank into interior forest and pleasant darkness, shielded from the hot afternoon sun by a canopy of oak and maple. I remembered to speak. "I think so," I said.

"You have got to come back—it's like a funeral home here. You've been on the road too long. You're only forty-five minutes away."

"I was under the impression you and Helen weren't speaking," I said.

"Dad," Henry said, "don't change the subject."

"Elwyn," my wife said in the background, "I did not tell Henry to call you. You know I wouldn't, even if I wanted to."

"Mother," Henry said, "we haven't gotten to you yet."

"What was it?" I asked. "A month or two ago?"

"What was what?"

"When you and Helen broke off the engagement."

"Nine months and three days."

"What are you two talking about?" Ettie asked.

"I suppose you just happened to know Helen was working for the telephone company today. When did she start this job?"

"We see her family every week in church," Henry said. "I talk to her brothers."

"So this call was only an excuse," I said, laughing. "A clever ruse to lure your ex-fiancée into talking, with an emotional issue as bait: father forced to travel for his job for months on end without food or congenial company."

"It was not," Henry said.

"Was she sympathetic? I mean, about your reasons for bothering her in the middle of such a busy important job."

"Of course she was. You know how much she adores you."

"So did it work?" I asked.

Henry finally laughed. "Yes. We're meeting tomorrow at Hitchcock's Drugstore in Dinkytown."

"What's going on here?" Ettie asked. "Who's meeting who?"

Henry put the phone against his chest. Muffled

sounds came over the line. My wife is very intelligent, but sometimes she just refuses to listen. Unreasonably, I wanted her to follow this conversation with only Henry's half as guide. Henry came on again.

"So when do you come home tonight?" he asked.

"I have to be in Le Sueur in an hour. I think they're having trouble with short-circuit beetles in one of the processing plants."

"So come home after that," Henry said. "We're having lamb."

I thought about this.

"What's a short-circuit beetle?" Henry asked.

"*Bostrichidae.* They seem to be attracted to the wheat chaff on the floors, but they eat anything, even through lead casings, to the wire. All the machinery keeps breaking down and no one can find the problem. The short-circuit beetles are only a theory of mine."

"Why are they attracted to wire?"

"Not wire. The insulation inside the lead casing. They have an electrifying dessert after the main course."

To the accompaniment of splashing water and Henry's laughter I heard my wife say, "Henry, why do you humor him? He makes our lives miserable and you laugh at his jokes and talk shop."

"What's that noise?" I asked. "Is she doing dishes this late in the afternoon?"

"From lunch," Henry said. "You see how bad

things are?" Ettie served lunch promptly at noon each day. It was two-thirty.

"You'd better put your mother on."

The field biology class was returning up the bridle path. Students waved as they passed, but I was distracted by the associations the phrase "bridle path" called up: bridal, threshold, the way marriage cut a path through dense forest.

"Elwyn?" my wife said shyly.

"Let me try to explain again."

"Are you seeing another woman?" she asked, in the same soft, shy voice.

"Mother," Henry said.

"Hold your tongue, young man," she said.

"Tell Henry to leave the room," I said and she did. After a long pause, in which I felt I could hear my wife's thoughts, I told her I felt another nervous breakdown coming on.

"Overwork brought on the other ones, so you should come home immediately, you will come home."

"No," I said. "I feel fine out here. It happens when I'm home. I wake up in the middle of the night and the house seems to be breathing, not me."

"Elwyn, you're enjoying yourself! We suffer here like Europeans and you traipse along the highway having a fine time."

I saw the woods around me, the seductive light, the beetles crawling into flowers' intimate parts. "No I

don't. This is hard work. I like it no more than you
do, but I can't do a job badly."

"You're so near," she said. "It's been weeks."

"It's been ten days." I stopped to consider the
childish fears of home beside the equally childlike
pleasure of these escapes into the woods. "Ettie, I
walk up the steps on our front porch and I see the
dust in the sunlight. It feels as if I'm entering a grain
elevator which is about to explode."

"Come in by the side door," Ettie whispered.

I could not tell if this was common sense or another example of my wife's literal-mindedness I found
both so endearing and infuriating.

"What am I doing wrong?" she said, choking.

"It's not you," I said, wrenched by how easily we
misunderstood each other. "I can't seem to explain."

"Yes you can," she said. "I am no longer pretty.
I'm not young anymore." She slapped something, a
fly on her arm perhaps, and for an instant I could see
her still attractive figure standing beside the smoked
glass cabinet, her face a muddy reflection, her back
bathed in the hot afternoon sun that pours into the
kitchen.

Then she spoke and her image disappeared. "Do
you remember the trip to Vancouver we took after
your last breakdown? You didn't say a word the entire
trip, just let your head bounce against the train window. I could tell you were alive only by the breath
that formed on the glass. But I didn't mind. In Van-

couver, at the Finnemores', you walked twenty miles a day so you would exhaust yourself to sleep at night. The first day you went back to work in Calgary was the hardest day of your life."

"I remember," I said. But I have no memory of this period, so I rely on other people's versions of these dreamlike incidents. A janitor found me the morning after my collapse and said, "You were sprawled out there on the lab floor as if you'd passed out. But get this, you had neatly folded your glasses beside you."

Ettie asked, "But do you remember how sweet it was to come home after that first day back at work? I've never seen anyone so happy."

I'd forgotten. The smell of French toast and bacon. My younger son, Greg, flying about the living room with his arms as propellers, oblivious of my ridiculous, triumphant return.

I asked how Greg's arm was.

"Why on earth do you want to know that?" Ettie said.

This happened three years ago, I realized with a shock. Greg had used his left arm as a propeller walking to school one day and the arm simply snapped. He hadn't hit anything. The bone was congenitally weak. He found his brother a few minutes later and said, "I think I hurt my arm." Henry, who is nearly a decade older, saw the bone jutting out of Greg's shirt and sent him home. "Why did you let him go alone?" I had asked Henry, horrified, but vaguely aware I might have done the same thing myself. "He knew the way," Henry had answered, sobbing.

"I've called the minister," Ettie was saying. "He'd be glad to come over any time tonight."

The minister was twenty-seven years old and unmarried. He arranged debates between me and the fundamentalist crowd on evolution. "He's young enough to be our son."

"Nonsense," Ettie said. "Both his parents died in that awful plane crash in La Crosse."

There was no disputing this logic.

"I've put fresh sheets on the guest bed if you—"

"Ettie," I said, "I'm not trying to avoid you."

"Then what *are* you doing?" she said tartly.

This made me pause. I could hear traces of other conversations over the line. Other husbands and wives trying vainly to stay in love.

"You missed dinner at the Akers'," Ettie said. The accusing tone of the first half of this sentence softened to guilty pleasure at gossiping the last half.

"I'm glad you went anyway."

"How did you know? Bob Aker picked me up, but then I recalled Helen's parents had promised to drive me. You remember Helen's parents, Jean and Jack?"

"Of course," I said. "I saw someone who looked just like Jack this morning at breakfast in La Crosse. He made an unpleasant impression on me." It wasn't the face of the cook's father as much as his manner, which reminded me of Jack.

"Did he now? Well, when Jean and Jack arrived, Jean suggested I drive with Jack so she could go with Bob Aker. She wanted to see how a Cadillac felt. Of course, you know Jack, he was furious. He didn't say a word to me the entire trip to Golden Valley. I tried to keep a conversation going, but it was like talking to a pig in mud, all grunts and groans."

"I like it when you talk dirty," I said.

"I do not. Where was I? Oh, at dinner Jack continued sulking, except in a crowd it became both more embarrassing and less noticeable. But Jean recognized it the moment Jack and I walked in the door, and periodically she would take him aside and whisper fiercely in his ear. But he never changed. The poor woman. Before dinner, he just sat by the antique gun case, staring straight ahead. Then at the table it was as if he wasn't there. He chewed his food and Jean tried to keep conversations going, but we could all see his behavior just ate away at her. Bob Aker once tried to involve Jack in the general chatter and said, 'The lumber business sure seems to be booming.' Jack's retort stopped the dinner talk cold."

"What did he say?" I asked, curious, but also there, in the Akers' sumptuous dining room, feeling the chilly pleasure of their hospitality.

"It wasn't what he said," Ettie replied in a quiet voice. "It was how he said it: 'We have nothing to complain about, but we're certainly not getting rich.'"

"He envies the Akers?" I said. "Well, anyone would."

"No," my wife said. "He's insanely jealous. It was Jean driving with Bob that set him off. But the most extraordinary part is that he apologized to all of us. Not that night, but by post the next day. Everyone got a humble letter. Mine said he was terribly embarrassed by his childish conduct. He was not sure his wife would ever forgive him. He said he was sorry he'd ruined an otherwise enjoyable evening."

"Ettie," I said, "this man's daughter may marry our son."

"Oh dear," she said. "And I heard from the Akers that Jean threatened to leave him once and for all. She's done it before."

"We could celebrate a marriage and divorce before the same justice of the peace."

"Do stop it," Ettie said. She paused. "I don't dislike Jack as much. It took courage to write those letters."

"It took a wife standing in the driveway, suitcases in hand."

"Of course he was wrong. He hardly ruined an enjoyable—just a moment there. What did you mean, this man's daughter might marry our son?"

"You're the one at home," I said. "Don't you see how Henry maneuvered this phone call? He wasn't doing it to reconcile his dear old parents."

"Oh Lord," Ettie said. "This phone call. We've been on for hours. We'll go to the poorhouse."

I reminded my wife of Helen's arrangement. "The phone company is paying for the call."

"Are you certain? I don't think it's right. Someone will find out."

"Ettie," I said, wanting to change the subject, "I miss you. I think I will come home tonight."

"Who could that be?" she said. "Someone's at the door."

"Fine," I said, angrily. "I'll hang up." The shadows on Route 19 had grown longer. The light of the interior forest had turned violet. I could do another tour of collecting on the bank of the river. A swallow zigzagged underneath the tent of leaves. But my wife had left the phone.

"I'll get it," I heard Henry cry.

I thought about hanging up, but curiosity and affection for this other interior kept me on the line. Our old house came alive again to my senses. The warm light from the kitchen that spilled into the foyer at a jagged angle. Ettie standing just beyond the light, like a superstitious cat, untying her apron strings. Henry bounding down the front stairs to intercept Greg at the door—an unknown head refracted by the stained glass of the door's porthole window. Somehow I knew who stood straightening her dress on the front porch. I heard Henry's high and cheerful voice; then it dropped an octave and I could feel my son blushing the way he always did when his emotions ran ahead of his ability to articulate them. Ettie spoke one or two indecipherable words, but she also fell silent. For a long moment there was no sound at all, except the tick of the Banff Hot Springs clock above the phone and the uphill chug of the refrigerator.

Ettie's whisper caught me off guard. "It's Helen. They've made up. You should see."

"I can," I said. "But I'm on my way home. I'll call Le Sueur from there."

"Well, if you want to," Ettie said dreamily. "But don't come home on my account."

Trapped by the current along the rim of a drainage system of the lake, where clots of weed and algae build up. Lake of the Isles, Minneapolis. July 5, 1957.

Whit Wheaton just relocated here to Minneapolis to become a vice-president at General Mills. We had known each other in Calgary. Twenty years ago he was shop foreman of the grain elevators owned by Robin Hood Flour, where I also worked. When they were settled, his wife called to invite us to dinner. My wife was surprised. "Why would they want to know us now? They make five times as much as you do." But at the dinner we remembered what good friends we were. After dessert the Wheatons asked about our church, and Ettie, who can be counted on to bring up embarrassing stories when she decides she's comfortable with new people, told about my Beetle Burlesque—grown men dressed in beetle costumes but with women's tights doing high kicks across the stage—for the children's home benefit show. The Wheatons joined the church anyway and within a month Whit was a deacon. In Calgary he had not been a churchgoer and often asked me to explain evolution to him. He was an outspoken opponent of Bible Bill Aberhart, the premier of Alberta who came to power the same time Hitler did.

Ettie became friendly with Whit's wife Lois again, but worried about her health. "Such a frail creature. She says not to ask about those years in Munich, where Whit was stationed after the war. But she seems to have become quite an expert on army doctors." In the parking lot after church one morning, Whit asked me to take him "bug collecting." He suggested Lake of the Isles, where they lived, the twisting lake bordered by neat lawns and tree-shrouded homes. "Afterward," he said, "we can play a little pool and sip iced tea over our catch."

I brought only a net and aspirator, not figuring to do much collecting. Many people are intrigued by the idea of this hobby, but few have any patience for the actual work. When I met him at his door, Whit wore a plaid shirt and high rubber boots. Out of his three-piece suit, he looked much younger than forty-five.

He tapped his boot. "I thought you might want to go wading." We must have looked quite a sight walking down the street toward the lake path. I told him the story of being chased out of a field in Apple Valley. The woman in her nightgown with a shotgun had shouted, "Go back to the state hospital where you belong." Whit did not laugh, but asked me exactly what it was I did with these insects. When I began to explain, he interrupted me. "Say, do you remember old Willy Twyman up at Calgary? He's at General Mills now—still couldn't pour piss out of a boot with the instructions printed on its heel, but he's got his own department. Who'd have thought the kid who demolished a grain elevator all by himself . . ." Whit trailed off.

In 1936, a grain elevator exploded. Twyman had been seen with a lit cigarette a few yards from an open door. Miraculously, no one was killed, and Whit had organized a company picnic near the smoking ruin. Explosions of that sort were common—we had not yet learned how to free the air of highly flammable grain dust—but the picnic was a brilliant idea. It provided enough manpower to keep the smoldering in check and turned the disaster into a festive affair. But Whit's picnic was also reckless. The two other nearby grain elevators were like ticking bombs, ready to go off at the slightest spark. Letting children romp around the tractor sheds was a heartless risk. I asked Whit about that picnic, if his intentions had been as subtle as they appeared. "I'd forgotten about that," he said, chuckling. "But hell, you may not remember, we were supposed to have a company picnic down by the Bow River that day. I just moved the location."

Dead fireworks littered the grass. Whit picked one up. "Quite a holiday. Are you an American citizen yet?" I said I wasn't. There was always the chance I'd be transferred back to Canada. "That's no way to think, man. You're master of your own fate. Don't do what the company tells you, tell the company what to do." I said I preferred to remain Canadian. Whit pondered this, absently bowing to elderly women we passed. All gave wide berth to my net. "You know, I shouldn't say this about my old company. We had high hopes for you. You had brains. A scientist, a good churchman, great with people. The lunks who ran Robin Hood knew nothing about buying wheat or processing flour. For years they resisted the idea of isolating vitamins—then look what happened." What happened was my department was assigned the job, under typical rush conditions. I worked day and night for months. I fed my own children foul-tasting early models of ascorbic acid. "Where was your ambition, old man?" Whit asked. "You could have owned Robin Hood." I said Robin Hood had ruined my life for twenty years. I had had a nervous breakdown. I wasn't a good father or husband. I had no ambition other than to survive. "I'm not criticizing you, Farmer. It wasn't your fault. The company should have used you better. But still—the place was ripe."

We sat on a wall of the old dam at the lower end of the lake. Water gurgled into a large drain directly below us. The river that once ran from the lake now flowed into the city's storm sewer system. I felt humiliated by this younger, more powerful man; my hobby's childishness and my life in his business exposed for what it was, without ambition. But the sensation of talking to a drunk nagged me—or the late nights trapped by the countless salesmen I traveled with who always had their lives to confess.

"After the war," Whit said, "you know, in Germany, with the occupation forces, I supervised the relocation of refugees in conjunction with the Red Cross. You do a smashing job, they've got this junior executive position waiting for you when you return from Europe. I was good at the job. Someone had to do it and I turned out to be best qualified, though I wouldn't have thought so beforehand. Officer training makes you use your head. I worked with my back in Calgary, didn't like to think of myself as a manager. But in this army job I realized indeed I was executive material. I believe I helped the vast majority of people who came through our office. It was easy with an army staff. It's near to impossible to do a good job with civilians—still I make do. What troubles me now is I can remember the face of almost every person I interviewed—or supervised the interview of. I see them as I fall asleep. It's uncanny. Must have something to do with the fact that we used translators so often—so I stared into their faces, looking for honesty, trying to root out the liars. I had to send people back to Hungary, Rumania, Russia. Who knows what I sent them to. In Russia they may have been executed as spies. Taste of western life. But I'm not the one with the conscience, my wife likes to say. Lois had two nervous breakdowns there. It was touch and go, but we pulled through."

Two boys began throwing a football on the field next to us. Whit twisted around and watched, slapping his thighs at good catches. One pass completely overshot its receiver, landing a few yards from us, and Whit leaped to his feet to retrieve the ball. He examined its laces a moment, laughed and signaled the boy farther away to start running, then launched a mighty pass. Something popped and Whit grabbed his throwing arm at the shoulder. The momentum of the catch carried the boy into Lake of the Isles Boulevard, where he dodged two cars like linebackers, then ran right into an old Packard coming from the other direction. The car was not moving fast and the boy was able to roll over the hood. Whit reached the scene in several giant strides; his right arm flapped like an empty shirt sleeve. My view of what happened next was obscured by the Packard, which had skidded to a stop. When I arrived, the boy was leaning over Whit, who lay twisted on the grass. The other boy laughed and said, "Whooee, some pass, Mr. Wheaton."

I asked the boy who'd rolled over the Packard if he was all right. He shrugged and smirked at the driver, who had rushed to the curb. The boy's left leg twitched, but he was evidently restraining the urge to rub it. Whit groaned. "Go down for a pass, kid," he said, and the boys laughed. "Dislocated my arm," Whit informed me as we helped him to his feet. "It'll hurt like hell tomorrow, now it's only killing me." Then his eyes rolled and he passed out. The boys, strong young teenagers, began to lift him. I didn't think it was wise, but they were neighbors. "We know him," they said. I walked alongside, with my net. He began to come to. His pulse was down but not dangerously low. "So?" he said. "It's thirteen a year. No more moves, no more refugees." He was offering me a job at General Mills, I realized, so to calm him I said I'd take it. He clenched my elbow with astonishing strength. His wife Lois was waiting at the front door as if she expected us. "What have you caught there?" she asked me in a jolly voice. Then she whispered, "Lay him on the pool table, boys. I'll get some milk, and Elwyn, you call the doctor."

"I'll be right with you," Whit shouted as they carried him down the stairs.

Larvae of Nicrophorus marginatus *uncovered on well-preserved corpse of field mouse, loosely covered with dirt in small pit. Faribault, Minnesota. July 9, 1957.*

"How could you go out on a day like this?" shouted my wife from the front porch. The old elm blocked my view of her. I had stopped the car and rolled down my window, thinking she had more instructions for shopping. But she simply restated her unhappy question, which had nothing to do with the weather. It was a beautiful summer day, the smell of thundershowers hanging in the air. The car started at my touch, and when I drove past the house I saw my older son, Henry, stooping over his small mother. After two months of agonizing delay, Henry got word yesterday that he had been awarded his Ph.D. in philosophy. Likely he was philosophically reassuring his mother, "Dad has his own way of mourning." Whit Wheaton hanged himself the day I took him collecting. Three days later my sister Ruth broke up several dozen barbiturate pills into a harmless mixture of milk and coffee-flavored liqueur and died in her stupefied sleep.

Faribault is fifty miles south of Minneapolis. It must have been seven o'clock when I passed the forest I wanted: thin rows of marsh, as if hoed out by a tractor. Boys had laid cast-off two-by-fours in a makeshift boardwalk to a pond a few dozen yards into the woods, a pond completely surrounded by leafy maple and sumac. I set to work without thinking, or with thoughts detached from the minute and complex activities this hobby involves. I was happy to find *Nicrophorus marginatus* larvae, which feed on dead rodents. The adults tunnel underneath the carcass, or drag it to loose dirt, and bury it—hence the name, Burying Beetle. Adults mate on the carrion underground, and the eggs remain there. The cover of earth keeps the carcass fresh and free of maggots that can survive only in open air. Because their meals are planned for months in advance, the larvae have the leisure to grow into full-fledged adults without the aboveground anxieties of the hunt or the hunted.

Whit hanged himself over the pool table I last saw him lying on, with an arm out of its socket. Looping the rope through pipe eight feet above the table must have caused excruciating pain, even using only his good arm. The coroner's assistant I met marveled at Whit's determination. This young man, fresh out of medical school, stood on the pool table to show me how Whit would have had to use both hands. "I just don't agree with the official report," he said. "It says he tied a weight to one end of the rope and threw it over. But I saw no sign of a weight. The coroner's office is always trying to make suicides look less heroic than they sometimes are."

Ettie and I had Whit's wife Lois over to dinner last night when the phone call came from my sister's husband in Detroit. Ettie's initial response to the news of Ruth's death should have given me a clue. My wife usually speaks in regular rhythms on the telephone, using the same deeply confidential tone no matter what the occasion or caller. This time she stood in the kitchen a moment, completely quiet. The next moment she was speaking a jet of words. Then she hung up and returned to the living room before I realized it. She told me later the instant she heard my brother-in-law's tone she decided not to upset Lois any more than she already was. My wife asked if we could call him back. My sister's husband was in no shape to talk by that point and had many more calls to make. Ettie told us it was only routine questions about stocks he wanted us to buy. "As if we had the money." She laughed. Lois said, "No, no. Call him back. I wouldn't want to be a bother." My wife has such an aversion to lying she blushes on the rare occasions she has to stray from her strict intuition of the truth. Fortunately I have no intuition at all and took Ettie's reddening as a sign of fatigue with Lois or annoyance with my brother-in-law, who had invested a good deal of other people's money in bad schemes. So I joked with Lois about the dull phone style of my sister's husband, which I mimicked, using exactly my wife's mannerisms. I concluded that it was infinitely more pleasing to talk with Lois in the flesh.

My son arrived bubbling over with his good news just as we were putting Lois into her car. Recognition took a moment to sink in on both sides. They had not seen each other since 1944. Lois could not have children herself and early on in our acquaintance adopted Henry as a surrogate son. Whit and Henry were famous hiking and fishing companions, but when Whit left for the war Henry took to "looking after" Lois, who has always been a handsome woman. I teased Henry on the subject of this infatuation—he couldn't have been more than fourteen—until the day he flew into a rage, screaming about our patriotic duties on the home front and Hitler's march into the Low Countries. Lois and Henry's reunion last night affected us all. My son had not been told of Whit's death, so at first we talked on top of each other about Henry's doctorate, his young wife Helen's beautiful singing voice, his children, or fifteen-year-old gossip. Then Henry noticed Lois was wearing a formal black gown, with a black shawl, and he asked, rather light-heartedly, whether there had been a death in the family.

Lois surprised me by holding up well during the ensuing revelation, which flattened Henry. He kept repeating, "I didn't have time to see him," as we returned to the house, and Lois kept saying, "Whitney always said you would go far in this world." We sat on the patio in the back yard. Henry's presence changed Lois, her maternal instincts surfacing to protect him from grief. But she also seemed younger and somewhat flirtatious. Earlier in the

evening she had not mentioned a word of the suicide
or events that might have led up to it. Now she explained everything—Whit's fear of aging, his terrible insecurity on the job, his rage against change—
and Lois proved her basic stability and common sense,
what had always endeared her to us. It was a long
evening. The moon set over the Honigers' garage in
the alley before we broke it up. We put Lois to bed in
the guest room, and then Ettie gave me the news of
my sister's death.

I pieced together the delicate pattern of incidents
—phone call, coffee, Henry's arrival—and gradually
fell in love with my wife all over again. Her heroic
reserve throughout the night of talk about one man's
life and death, while withholding her own painful
knowledge, filled me with a strange longing for her.
Naturally, my reaction bewildered Ettie, but she was
not shy, only careful. "Lois is just next door," she
said. "Wasn't she lovely tonight? Shh." This morning, when Ettie began to pester me about planning
the trip to Detroit for my sister's funeral, I reminded
her of her extraordinary performance the night before—keeping quiet about Ruth's death—and she
was flattered into confused retreat.

The woods came to life after a few moments of the
terrified calm my presence provoked. A beaver sur-
faced in water I had thought was forest floor clover.
The ripples she created showed the extent of the
pond, whose edge lay only a few feet from me. I must

have been sitting very still on my log, for when I coughed the beaver jumped straight out of the water. Her tail slapped the startled pool and sent a spray of weeds over me. I sniffed skunk cabbage. As a boy I had cleared a skating rink in the forest off our farm in Manitoba. When my sister Ruth and I skated in the late winter the only smell was this perfume of decay, skunk cabbage. Ruth made me skate-dance with her early one morning after her fiancé was killed in the First World War. The British shamelessly used Canadian units as cannon fodder on the front lines. My sister hugged me as we danced, and she laughed at the awful odor that naturally brought death in France to her mind. It reminded me that spring was near, and I timidly informed her the songbirds would be arriving soon. We spent many a day in the melting snow counting redwings, bronzed grackles, and fox sparrows, and gravely writing down our findings. But Ruth said, "We were man and wife," which frightened me. I was thirteen, she was sixteen. I thought she was referring to us. My greatest wish was to live with Ruth all my life, as Wordsworth had lived with his sister. Then she laughed. "Not you, dummy. Him. France."

Whit interferes with these memories of my sister, even the involuntary, sour ones. I have not seen Ruth in two years, and little of her since the second marriage and heavy drinking. The first recognition of Ruth's alcoholism came with a rotten citrus smell in their apartment that made me strangely giddy. Naïvely I asked what it was, a household cleaner of some sort? But it was Ruth, the poison breathing out her skin. We both blushed without saying a word. Now Whit's famous rescue of me and Willy Twyman nudges in, also triggered by that smell of rancid grapefruit. Twyman and I had gone down to one of the experimental fields near Calgary. This was 1937, the day was warm—a chinook blowing up from Montana—but late November. We were out in the far field taking soil samples and winter wheat about two miles from the car. The test tubes of chemicals Twyman was afraid to handle preoccupied me so much I didn't notice the heavy clouds building. Twyman had noticed but did not think they held snow. In less than an hour a foot of it fell and the temperature dropped thirty degrees. The air had been so warm, Twyman complained. His car wouldn't start and he panicked. He began to cry, stamping his feet. I remembered a tiny shack up the dirt road a way where we had a better chance of surviving. I left some rocks on the hood of the car forming an arrow that pointed in the direction of the shack.

Whit arrived within two hours, and Twyman hugged him, blubbering. Whit turned to me, breathing heavily. "Don't I get a kiss from you too?"

"You're drunk," I said, my terror finally organizing itself into one moment of idiotic outrage.

"Of course I am." He laughed. "Think I'd risk my

neck on a stunt like this if I hadn't a few beers under my belt?" His breath stung my nostrils as we embraced, and forever after the smell flooded me with sudden elation.

Nitidulids *in fermenting oranges in garbage dump. Highway 14 outside Palmdale, California. April 6, 1961.*

I was about fifty yards away, watching the kangaroo mouse through binoculars. He hopped a few yards, then stopped, stiff with fear. A moment passed and so did his fear. He began to clean himself, washing off the embarrassment of a false alarm. Then he stood on hind legs to yawn, one paw raised, the other curled against his chest. For this instant he looked like a little boy I know after he's been caught in mischief. The next instant I saw the blur of a shadow and the talons of a hawk slicing cleanly through the head of the mouse, one claw popping out his eye. The field glasses fell against my hip and frantically I searched the sky with my own eyes. A buteo hawk wheeled away over the foothills of the San Gabriel Mountains. My grandson Stephen had sidled up to me and wanted to look through the binoculars. "Now that you're done with them," he said. Such a bright sun hung in the bronze sky I worried the five-year-old would look directly into it, burning his retinas. "Please," Stephen said quietly, old enough to know that by modulating his whirlwind behavior to this occasional oasis of calm he made me a slave to his requests. But when I freed the crinkled leather straps from my shirt collar and turned to hand him the field glasses, he was gone. He was racing after his little sister across a matrix of tiny ravines. Evie had discovered a pile of rocks Stephen was storing for his own future use.

Two of the three grandchildren were under our care today at this scenic view rest area in the Mojave Desert. The elder boy had accompanied his parents to Disneyland. Stephen and Evie were too young for that excitement. Ettie, who was unpacking a picnic lunch near the car, kept Stephen from swooping down on his sister with a deft command: "Come help me unload this heavy tin of cookies." We had been weekend parents of these alert, healthy children in Minneapolis, before we moved to Montreal and our son's family moved to San Jose. Perhaps it was ridiculous to miss them so much, to risk my job for this cross-country drive. ("We don't normally let our people just up and take a month off," the general manager said the day before I left, as if I had not given him three months' warning and trained a capable replacement who would be taking over my job in a few years anyway.)

With a shortbread cookie in hand, Stephen came running back toward me, but he tripped. A spectacular feet-over-shoulders somersault ended with the boy on one knee, miraculously upright on a patch of soft sand only a few yards from me. My grandson looked to me for his own reaction in the breathless instant after the tumble. Ettie clapped a hand over her mouth and jerked little Eva to her side. But it was over, and betraying the least fear would only have made the boy cry, so I laughed and Stephen did too.

"It's the Santa Ana wind," I shouted, pointing toward the desert. Ettie nodded, and a hand shot up to her forehead to rub away the imaginary headache. Our hosts in Anaheim had ominously warned us the hot dry wind was predicted for today. Violent quarrels erupted. Suicide rates climbed. Fires roared through the canyons. This wind had gotten under my wife's skin. "Do you suppose it's safe to go into the desert today?" she had asked in the car.

But on the horizon, later, I saw a charming scene through the field glasses. Near a saguaro cactus was a small, slight man in a three-piece suit. He was comfortably perched on a stool, though sometimes he seemed to float just above it, with something flat on his lap. He was sketching. A pile of paper lay about his feet, fluttering in the breeze like butterflies sunning themselves. The idea of this fellow appealed to me. I imagined he was a businessman who had stopped here on the way to an appointment. The drawing was something he preferred to shield from his colleagues. I compared my own hobby with his and felt an instinctive affection for this stranger one hundred yards away. I decided to pay the businessman-artist a visit.

Ettie endorsed a collecting trip. "You'll be out of my hair at least," she said. Stephen was equally unenthusiastic. Whenever he saw my net, his eyes grew wide with fear and he became very quiet. He joined me collecting only when his older brother did. "No, you don't get Grampa all to yourself," I heard him say once.

I carried our sleeping granddaughter into the back seat of the car. "Of course you won't be long," Ettie whispered, staring at the beautiful blond-haired girl, whose sleep was creased by an amazing frown from the hot wind.

"No more than an hour," I whispered back, teasing.

"What will we do for an hour?" she said out loud.

"Read a book." I laughed. "Change the oil in the car."

"You will be gone no longer than half an hour. The children are getting testy."

"Eva's asleep. Stephen is digging a tunnel to Disneyland."

"Good Lord," Ettie said. "Just go." Stephen stood up from his mining and walked to the picnic table, which was a few yards from us. He began to kick the stone leg of the bench.

"It's the Santa Ana wind," I said.

"Nonsense. You're a stubborn old man with a conscience like a sieve." Stephen put a palm to his forehead, an imitation of his grandmother I was just this moment in no mood to recognize, and he scanned the horizon with wide, terrified eyes.

"I'll just walk into that desert," I said quietly to my wife, torn between anger and the impulse to protect my grandson from fear. "I won't come back."

"You wouldn't dare," she said, but clearly she was taken in by the outrageous threat. Stephen caught Ettie's eye. "Oh there now," she said, gathering him into her arms. "After all these years, your grandmother still can't tell when your grandfather is kidding." Then she said to me, in a voice so gentle Stephen did not seem to notice its content, "Sometimes I could just shoot you." In fact, the five-year-old sighed at our apparent reconciliation.

"I won't be long," I said, picking my net off the picnic table.

"No longer than an hour," Stephen said.

I was distracted along the way, overturning rocks, cutting up fallen cacti. Eventually I reached the man in the business suit and found he had been watching me for some time.

"Buddy," he said, extending his hand. "But my

colleagues insist on giving everyone nicknames—
mine's Chicago, which I originally didn't care for,
but after all these years . . . Well, a nickname grows
on you no matter how awkward it is."

We shook hands and I saw one of the drawings on
the ground. A flat plain suggested only by a line. An
animal with oddly human gracelessness running very
fast, the speed conveyed by lines of air resistance and
specks of dust kicked up behind him. Buddy had been
watching my grandson.

I introduced myself and told Buddy I had not seen
a three-piece suit since Utah. Sports jackets seemed to
be the fashion in Southern California.

"That so?" he said, shielding his eyes from the sun
but also sizing me up as if for a drawing. "We began
wearing the suits as a joke. The producer came into
the studio one day with our paychecks—I'm a cartoonist, you see—and he says, 'Pee-yew, this place
smells like a farm,' so we all wore our Sunday best the
next time he came and I got accustomed to the feel.
I'm the only one who still wears the suit. Provides
occasional inspiration for the boys."

He sat down. "Mind if I draw?"

"Go right ahead," I said. I could see he was drawing my butterfly net. I asked if he was from Chicago.

"Hmm?" he said, his shoulders moving out of pro-
portion to the small line figures he was drawing.
"No. Around Milwaukee—Palmyra."

He finished his sketch. A complete picture, or enough to suggest one, in thirty seconds. It was not me holding the net, but a homely anteater who I could tell even at a glance was shy and rather depressed. Buddy spit on the ground and tore the sketch off the pad.

After a moment, I asked, "Why the nickname Chicago?"

"Hmm? Oh, I am sorry," he said. "Chicago is the Windy City. I have this reputation for talking nonstop, though you can see it's not always the case. Besides, these people look at a map and think, 'Milwaukee, Chicago, what's the difference?' Did you say Utah before? But you're not from Utah. I'd say Cincinnati. You have that pleasant Ohio Valley nasal block."

"No." I laughed. "We're from Montreal, but I've been moved around a bit. We're visiting relatives in San Jose now."

"Are those them?" he asked, pointing. Then he nodded at my binoculars, which I exchanged wordlessly with him for the drawing board and charcoal pencil.

"Two of the three grandchildren and my wife," I said.

"Handsome woman," he said. "I'm no good with kids." His eyes betrayed another drift toward distracted musing. We returned to his "studio."

"I'll just putter around," I said.

"Please. Make yourself at home."

Ten minutes later he shouted, "Elwyn, come over here." I did. "When I get stuck on a character," he said, "I like to discuss it with myself out loud. I didn't want to embarrass you by launching into one of these monologues without warning. You're standing there plain as that bug on your pants, but I'm stuck."

"You want to talk me onto paper?"

"You see," he said, on top of my question, "we draw movement, but you can't *draw* movement, you have to map it out, which demands something artists are not accustomed to doing—thinking." He laughed for an instant, but his hand came flapping up in front of his mouth the way people's do when they've eaten hot food. "But listen, listen"—I'd made no move to speak—"we've got all this stuff— motion, transition, the magic of personality revealing itself in the simplest movements. Now you, Elwyn, you have this funny habit of hitching up those ugly pants just as you settle into one of your crouches. Lot of us older guys do that, but something about your mannerism amuses me . . . Of course! It's this ghost of a curtsy with the fingers."

Buddy stood up to demonstrate. On him the ges- ture looked ridiculous, but I recognized myself in it, and I laughed.

"No," Buddy said abruptly. "That's not enough. A

little curtsy only vaguely characterizes you. You know, in those work clothes you look like a grizzled gas station attendant, not a professor." He saw I was about to speak but cut me off with a slice of the hand.

"No, wait. A few minutes ago I saw you lying at the base of one of those huge cacti. Why were you poking up its innards?"

I told him the saguaro had been dead for some time.

"Doing an autopsy? All right, fine. But you lay there as if you were in bed. You flipped over to get something from your bag and it was like those flip-flops we do in our sleep when the arm goes flying over the wife's mouth, only it's not the wife in bed— it's the man next door who's wandered into the wrong house. Okay, okay."

He began to draw again, the wide bowl around us and another low butte off in the distance. But a series of low groans made his dismay with even these pre-liminaries obvious. I wondered if I was distracting him.

"I'm not in your way?" I asked.

"No, no. I'll just be a moment."

Then he looked up, a grin slowly spreading across his face.

"That's . . . very . . . good," he said, scribbling something down on the pad, shorthand lines and squiggles, not words or a sketch. "I like it. 'I'm not in

your way?' You have just put four days of work in the
wastebasket."

"I'm sorry," I said.

"Don't be, no, no. You've given me the only good
idea I've had all month. Our hero is collecting butterflies. The villain is painting landscapes. The
villain keeps finding the hero has turned up on his
canvas. Every time he starts a new landscape, there's
the butterfly net again, the round head blocking this
exaggerated ideal of nature he has. It drives him
crazy."

The next moment Buddy was cleaning up his work
area, jerking here and there, kneeling and jumping to
his feet again as if he were fifteen years old. He apologized. "I get very nervous when I stumble on a good
idea, they're so rare these days." Soon we were walking briskly to the picnic grounds. He had put on a
spotlessly white cowboy hat, which made him look
even smaller than he was.

"You don't suppose you could give me a lift back to
the studio?" he asked. "It's just off the highway over
the hills."

"How did you get here?" I asked.

"A driver brought me out. He has strict instructions not to pick me up for another two hours. I don't
work unless I know I'm stranded."

Then Buddy gave a hurried, incoherent history of
the cartoon industry, speaking as if I were an insider

familiar with all the terms of art. He finished with this anecdote: "They keep cutting back our budgets. There's a story about Jack Warner. He was doddering around his big office. Every year he signed an enormous check of money over to us. But one year he said to his treasurer, just as he was about to sign, 'I love that Mickey Mouse. Tell them to do more shorts with him.' The treasurer said, 'I don't believe Mickey Mouse is with us.' The budget got slashed."

Buddy was laughing uncontrollably, wiping tears from his eyes, when Stephen came running up to us. He stopped five feet short, sensing there was something to mistrust in my companion.

I told the boy this man made the cartoons we watched on Saturday morning.

"We drove in the car Saturday morning," Stephen said. Buddy reached out to pat the boy's head, but Stephen ducked away, grabbing my belt loops on his orbit around me.

"You see I'm a wash with children. A cartoonist who scares every child he meets!"

My wife arrived, Evie in her arms. Buddy lifted his hat and introduced himself, brightening. "Your husband tells me what a saint you are to put up with his beetles in the icebox, on the kitchen table, in the oven."

Ettie laughed at this unreal picture of our home life, then flatly contradicted him. "Mind you, I keep him out of the kitchen. I give him free rein in the basement. But if I catch so much as one bug crawling up those stairs."

"But you don't mind joining him on his field trips and holding his extra net for him?"

My wife found this image even more amusing. "Sometimes he takes me to a French hairdresser over by Dorion, and he goes to a little park by the river, especially if I'm to have a set. She's a French girl, but she's very good."

"You don't seem to be suffering any at the hands of our California stylists," Buddy said.

My wife was won over completely by this stranger, so I told her Buddy was a cartoonist.

"A what?" she said, frowning for a moment. Now that both of her sons had settled into their careers— Greg a pilot and Henry a professor—few other jobs met with her immediate approval.

"Bugs Bunny," Stephen said, by way of explanation.

"Yes," Buddy said cautiously to the boy. "He's one of my employees."

"He is?" Stephen's mouth fell slightly open. "Do you *talk* to him?" He let go of my belt loops.

"Only his agent. Put Bugs in front of a camera, and he's the nicest bunny you'd ever want to meet. But he can be a little particular when the lights go dim."

"I see," Stephen said. "Where did you find him?"

"It's a long story, Stevie."

"Stephen," the boy corrected him. Then my grandson turned to me and said, "The strange man is not telling the truth."

The tentative smile disappeared from Buddy's lips.

"I beg your pardon," he said, visibly shaking. "If you want, I can give you and your family a tour of the studios. Your grandfather kindly offered me a ride back to the city."

"We don't have room," Stephen said. The finality of this pronouncement silenced all three adults for a moment, making us forget a five-year-old had uttered it.

Then I had the bright idea of using the recurring theme of our conversations today and said, "Remember the Santa Ana wind, Stephen. We don't want to leave the poor man alone in this weather."

Stephen's eyes bulged as they scanned the horizon, and I immediately regretted my tactic—each time we discussed this subject he grew more frightened.

"Elwyn," Ettie said savagely, "you see how your teasing harms the children."

Near tears, Stephen said bravely, "No, Gramma, I like Grampa to scare me with jokes."

*Limulodidae sifted from ant nest and taken off
backs of ant hosts. Horseshoe Beetles feed off
excretions of ants, sometimes a threat to colonies, but
sufficient numbers in this case to indicate they are
performing some useful function. Next to James
Bay, ten miles below tundra. Akimiski Island,
Northwest Territories. August 6, 1961.*

Over the lab intercom at work they had called my
name. We were building a giant grain funnel de-
signed to accelerate flow down the chutes of grain
elevators. The general manager's secretary was rush-
ing out of the office. "Your brother's on the phone,"
she said. My brother Eli had not spoken to me since
1958, when he asked to borrow $300. Thirty years ago
he stole my life savings from the bottom of my mother's upright dresser. I would have entered my second
year of graduate school in entomology that fall, but
instead I found a job with the same company I work
for today. Eli has called occasionally the last few years
to ask for small loans, as if to prove I still forgive him.
He also calls Greg, ostensibly to talk about his fledg-
ling flying career, but my son passes on the news he
knows Eli wants me to hear. I was happy to learn this
time Eli was calling simply to order me to fly north
with him to an island in James Bay. My wife was
visiting her Canada full of sisters for the month. I had
been looking forward to a quiet weekend, maybe fix
the lawn mower, finish building boxes for the ama-

teur entomologist exhibit at the Montreal Museum of Natural History.

Eli talked over the engine roar of his seaplane. Then in the long subarctic twilight we drank whiskey on the cabin porch, the Grumman Goose groaning against its mooring lines one hundred yards away. "Drink, so I don't drink it all myself," Eli said. I don't usually drink, but I said I'd have one glass to help me sleep through the midnight sun. "Same old Elwyn," he said. He was gone when I awoke at six. "I'm color blind and they want me to look for a camouflaged army hut near Fort Severn," his note said. *"Bright* green, they promised. I'll be back by five. If you hike, wear my orange hunting vest, which scares off polar bears. Make noise. The flag on top of this cabin can be seen for miles if you go inland. Bring binoculars." I had never been to this cabin, which Eli shared with two other bush pilots for hunting, but I often camped in the wild. He enjoyed ribbing me as if I were just a city boy.

At six-forty a ripple of thunderclaps shook the cabin. From the front door I saw nothing. The sound reminded me of the wind tunnel we use at work, when its jet engine turbines started up. Not at all like a small propeller plane, which is what I suspected— Eli buzzing me. He had said the nearest neighbor was at the other end of the island, forty miles away. I put out the fire and packed gear for a hike, thinking I had imagined the noise. When it happened again I was in the outhouse and pushed the door open to see the five-foot forest of pines flopping in every direction. But the sound vanished, or blended into the mosquito buzz and gurgle of a nearby stream. It came in rapid pulses, with a steady machine whine underneath the pulses. Needless to say, I did not make good use of the outhouse.

The streambed was fifty paces down a gulley from the cabin. "Follow it and you'll find the blackest ocean you've ever seen," Eli had told me. I carried my sifter, net, and the binoculars. The balsam fir grew no taller than my head this far north. But because the climate stunted them, not altitude or wind, they had the full-bodied appearance of trees ten times their height, and I felt a bit like Gulliver limping alongside their tops. James Bay was a very dark blue. Eli had remembered a tall tale our father once told us as children. We were tracing our fingers over the map of Canada. I came to James Bay and Eli asked Father, "Was it named after you?" Father was also a James, James Elwyn Farmer, and said, "I was an explorer in my youth," in his famous deadpan way. "But your mother made me give it up." At the time I suspected it was a joke, but I did not want to anger Father by questioning him. I researched the problem at the school library, and when I confronted him with the truth, Father laughed but applauded my industry. For ten years, however, Eli believed Father. "I didn't find out until high school," he shouted. "They took me for such a dunce."

A wall of fog spilled onto the black beach and rolled out to sea. From half a mile away it appeared solid enough to lean against. But inside, the only reminders were the stained horizon and the ghostly drip of condensation from an invisible plateau a few feet above my head. Marshes by the ocean created this phenomenon. Cold morning air passing over warm earth and water channeled the fog into a narrow belt. I set to work, laying out my sifter and white tarp. But every so often a strange feeling came over me, causing my neck to tingle. I thought I was being watched. Each time this happened I would also hear Eli's voice, as if he were a step behind me. I recognized the two sensations as symptoms of the nervous breakdowns I had had. I was prone to a sort of physical and mental closing-up-shop when overworked or under acute financial pressure, but I have not had an attack in ten years. A doctor warned me to regard the flashbacks as ripples after the splash, not the splash itself. But I now found myself talking out loud or surprised by fear. I climbed up to the marsh that was on the rise five feet above the bay. It would be an unlikely harbor for water beetles. Eli thought I was a fool to look for my bugs this far north. In the tropics, he could understand, where you had to wrestle insects to the ground. But in the tundra you hunt marten, moose, caribou, polar bear. "Mount one of them in a box of yours," he had said, laughing.

I had left my hand shovel at the cabin and stumbled down the bank to the beach to pick up a flat stick I'd seen that would do for a shovel. Eli said he was jealous of my one marriage. "Christ," he roared over the Grumman engine, "I'm just getting to know Gladys," his second wife. "You've had thirty years with the beauty queen." "Still," he said later, "I'm not sure I want to know Gladys all that well. Flying is my escape hatch when the show gets dull."

I had wanted to say I appreciated these spontaneous trips and envied him his mobility. When I traveled for the company it had always been by land, from hotel to hotel. My wife and I lived in five different cities from 1930 to 1960. The last move, to Montreal, was a terrible blow to Ettie, who had not slept a full night since we left Minneapolis. I had almost quit rather than transfer, but one of the vice-presidents invited me to his house on Lake Minnetonka for a drink and told me it was the Christian thing to obey one's company. Besides, my complicated pension plan, straddling the U.S. and Canada, would have been unworkable with any other company. A lawyer in our church said this was blackmail but not illegal. I wanted to say all this to Eli, but I couldn't make myself heard over the engine roar the entire flight. Eli had no trouble making himself heard. I found myself shouting at my reflection in the muddy pond, "You can hear me. Quit saying 'beg pardon.' "

My tarp began to flap in the breeze—a cold front moving in—so I put rocks on the windward side. "You've always had it so easy," my brother said, and my stick, digging into root under swamp muck, snapped in half. "I was nothing. I drank. At thirty-three, I still slept with whores while you were teaching Sunday school. I got my license to fly only because of a harebrained scheme to smuggle whiskey into the States. We were so stupid we didn't realize Prohibition had been repealed three years before." The bag of swamp soil emptied into the sifter. The sweet smell of manure alerted me to an intruder, perhaps bear or moose. The sun broke through ground fog over the short hills to the east, giving me light I needed for the magnifying glass I used to warm suspicious lumps of sifted dirt. If the hot light made the lump move, I sucked it into my aspirator to see what I'd caught. I was getting annoyed with this Eli in my mind. He had planned the weekend to avoid me as much as to see me. He would arrive tonight, probably hours late, and fall asleep moments after his one glass of whiskey. He is no more of a drinker than I am. He frightened me with his endless supply of resentment, but to be honest I knew I did nothing to improve our relationship. Being resented provided some small consolation for my own sense of frustration and failure. "I can't pass the color chart test anymore," he had said the night before. "I used to memorize them. But the mule of a French licenser in Port Arthur won't let me nick the tests beforehand anymore. Down south they don't use colored landing lights now, with all that fancy radar. Who cares if a bush pilot can't tell the difference between red and orange? They're going to take my license away from me."

Something boomed. Then the thunderclaps returned, at first soft, then louder and louder, and I saw the thing coming toward me along the beach. More booms, then rapid popping, and I looked toward the cabin. A coil of black smoke rose just to the right of its orange flag. The thing had halted in the air a few hundred yards from me. I could not remember its name. A hovering plane that kicked up a storm of black sand. I saw a man peering at me through binoculars, and the USMC logo on the thing's belly. It could have passed for two giant damselflies mating. I raised my own field glasses and saw a man with a shaved head wave. Then the machine darted toward me. The column of air it lifted tore my tarp from its rocks and I ran after the dancing white rectangle. "Hey, Pop," a voice shouted. "You Elwyn Farmer? Slow down."

The helicopter had landed. When the blades slowed and I could see again, I walked in a crouch to the young American marine and introduced myself. "Your brother got worried about you," he said. "He radioed us to pick you up. We couldn't make you out for a minute in that fog. I'm afraid one of our practice bombs landed a little near to your cabin. But don't worry, they're only smoke bombs. You sure can run for an old guy." He pointed to my tarp tangled in a bush. "What are you doing here?" he asked. I told him and asked what they were doing here. "This is a war game. We're fighting the army." I asked if he knew they were in Canada. The pilot, in dark glasses and headphones, laughed. "Damn, we're fighting the *Canadian* army. You think our own army could handle us?" Then he asked if I wanted a ride around the island. We flew over a beach just a mile away with hundreds of crawling soldiers and dozens of amphibious tanks. I used an extra set of headphones, so there was no need to shout over this engine. I asked to see the tree line. "You mean it ends?" the marine asked. I said my brother had not told me there would be a war on this island. The marine laughed. "Real son of a bitch. But quite a spread he's got." We saw how the green stubble of trees did suddenly end, giving way to yellow tundra, and I realized my brother had no other means of showing his angry affection for me than this island and the dangerous practical joke revoked at the last moment.

Five Hydrophilids *taken in a pool of rainwater*
about four feet in diameter and one inch deep in the
center; collected on blacktop of restaurant parking
lot. Pool accumulated from heavy rains during the
day. Pte. Claire, Quebec. August 11, 1965.

At one point a vice-president, who made it quite plain
he was angling to depose the president, began to
dance with him. Everyone in the private room at the
restaurant put down their drinks and stopped talking.
I was the only non-executive at the party, a fact
turned over in conversation all night long. "How did
Farmer slip through?" "Are you taking good notes?"
Seth Thomson, the president, had always liked me,
though in an absent-minded way that often made me
feel liked for elusive reasons which if pinned down
would probably not fit me at all. The evening was in
honor of Carton, who had been Thomson's sidekick
for thirty years. During the first toast, Carton joked
uneasily that this was more like a wake than a celebration. The mood had been quite festive, but in Carton's inadvertently penetrating manner he described
the underlying tone. The rumor was that Thomson
would be asked to retire in a matter of weeks.

The dancing began as an obvious effort by a new
man from Toronto to ridicule Thomson, who
had become drunk very quickly. But McHenry and
Thomson discovered they enjoyed the exercise and

made the accordion player speed up his waltz, and soon eight blue-suited couples were marching across the floor, bumping, falling, laughing like schoolboys.

I sat exempt from the dancing and chatted with Carton. The celebration was clearly something of a joke on him, but Thomson's affection for Carton was also genuine, the product of thirty years of shared memories. I think this was why no one tried to drag Carton onto the dance floor. But he winced each time a dancer grabbed one of our neighbors.

My own immunity from the dancing may have been the result of an unhappy incident early in the evening. Roaring like a bear, Thomson tried to make me drink a big mug full of beer. A crony stood behind me, laughingly holding back my arms. I said something sharp, I don't remember what, and Thomson's face fell. "Only a bit of pleasantry, Professor," he muttered. Carton had first used that nickname on me, although he was the one who deserved it, with his Ph.D. in agriculture. Carton told me later the boys were surprised to see how tough I could be on the president. As the night progressed, Thomson began calling me his "wet nurse." I believe it was during the dancing that I phoned my wife. She had already taken her sleeping pill. She was distantly amused by my descriptions and unperturbed that I might be home very late. "You just keep your flock in line," she said.

The maitre d' supervised the skeleton staff of wait-
ers and therefore suffered a good deal of harassment.
"Jean," someone would shout, pronouncing the
name the American way. "Gene, get over here with
that American bourbon" (he was not the Jean of
Chez Jean). Perhaps to vent his frustrations he turned
off the air conditioning for a few minutes every half
hour. I noticed this tactic when men began to exhale
clouds of vapor after sucking down their cold drinks.
I asked the maitre d' if the restaurant had recently
installed the air-conditioning system. "Yes," he said.
"You understand me! I do not trust it. You feel how
hot it is outside? It is not natural in here, like a meat
locker—or a morgue, no?" The maitre d' decided he
and I had "sympathetic" roles to play that evening, so
when I excused myself at two-thirty to take a walk,
the maitre d' told me with a grin that he would flick
off the floodlights twice as a signal if he needed my
help.

The St. Lawrence River, called Lac St. Louis at this
point, ran along a triangular parking lot behind the
restaurant. A narrow belt of cattails stood between the
river and the gravel. Sweat soaked my shirt moments
after I left the building, but the dense misty air was
preferable to the private dining room. Carton told me
it had been Thomson's idea to invite me, "to keep the
boys on their toes." Thomson probably meant nothing by this comment; he often teased Carton with

nonsense at the office to see how he transformed the nonsense into serious instructions or gossip. But there was a grain of truth in this nonsense.

I was leaning over the trunk of my car, too tired to pull out my net and collecting kit, wondering why I had remained at this party so long, when the floodlights went off. It was a moonless cloudy night, so I was plunged into complete darkness. I groped through parked cars as my eyes adjusted. When I cleared the last tail fin, a low voice said, "Farmer, come quick. Mr. Thomson is throwing up." It was Carton speaking. I tripped and landed on my knees. There was a scuffle. The lights came on, blinding me. I heard a vaguely familiar laugh. When I could see clearly again I recognized McHenry, the vice-president who had begun the dancing. He was alone in the doorway, his gray crew cut glistening. He said, "You're the one who collects beetles, eh?" I said I was, feeling my palms for scrapes. "You doing that right now?" When I passed him in the doorway, he laughed. "You looked pretty pathetic for a moment there."

Four executives were kneeling in front of the stand-up urinals in the long bathroom. The maitre d' held the door wide open, disgustedly yelling in French to his one remaining waiter to bring a mop. Another dozen executives and the accordion player sat at a round table not far from this door. They could plainly see each spasm and hear each retch. The accordion player fingered a spare, mournful tune. McHenry was by my side, his laugh like a hissing radiator. "Thomson went first," he said, "but he couldn't make it to a private stall. The other three didn't seem to think it would be good politics to use a stall if the president hadn't." Out of the corner of my eye I saw Carton, alone at another table, shivering. I walked over to him to escape McHenry, who made me nervous.

"McHenry is a fine fellow, isn't he," Carton said. "He's promised to come down to my little farm in Illinois." His "little farm" was a seventeen-acre private experimental field station often borrowed by the University of Illinois. "Of course, I hear McHenry has a mistress in Detroit, which may be why he'd want to visit me. The story is, he once took his sons to meet her, to see if they would consider accepting her as a stepmother. Now they won't talk to him."

A wave of shakes and chattering teeth came over Carton. I asked what was the matter. "N-nothing. I shouldn't drink, is all."

"You haven't had a drop the whole night," I said.

"No, oh no." Carton giggled. "I had two cups of coffee just now to stay awake. Caffeine and I don't mix."

The waiter had closed the bathroom door, but Thomson pushed it open, straightening his vest and tie. "Well, boys," he said in his booming voice to the main table, "where were we?" Then to me: "Won't you join us for one tiny drink, Professor?" I asked the maitre d' if he could fix Carton a hot toddy, and everyone laughed, a gentle friendly noise that sounded out of place in this raucous room. "Professor and I go way back," Carton said, red up to his ears.

Carton's tone of voice brought a story to mind. From 1952 to 1959 he had been my direct supervisor in Minneapolis. Late one summer I took a brief vacation to Christopher Lake in Saskatchewan. In passing, Carton had asked me where I was going. I got out a map. "They got people way up there?" he barked. (The table laughed at my simple imitation, and Carton himself beamed.) "Whatcha wanna go way up there for?" Carton had asked. I said the fishing was great and wondered out loud whether he wanted to join us. He had said, "Maybe I will, maybe I will," studying the map like a general in his bunker. At Christopher Lake a few days later, a teenage boy came huffing up to our cabin on his bike. He had ridden five miles from town. "Any of you Mr. Farmer?" he asked the porchful of brothers-in-law. I stepped forward. "You got a call in town, someone named Carton. He left a number." I drove the boy back. I thought Carton might be phoning from Prince Albert, having decided to visit after all, but the number I found in town was for our Minneapolis office. It took twenty minutes to patch the call through several cities. Finally, I reached the lab secretary, who did such good imitations of her boss herself. "Nope, nope," she said. "Carton just vanished into thin air. Here a minute ago. I could try to findum." She eventually did. Carton and I chatted a while, as if I were calling from across the street. "Good fishing?" he asked. I reminded him: "Drop an unbaited hook in the water—" "Yes, yes, but how's the weather? It's hot as the devil down here." "Warm, but cold at night. So why did you call?" I asked finally. "Call, call? *You* called me." I told him about the disruption of my routine, being ripped from the one-word-a-minute conversation with my brothers-in-law. "Why did I call you?" Carton asked himself. "I—I don't remember."

It's not one of my funniest stories, but this audience was receptive. It occurred to me they had been telling the same kind of story all night—about Carton, the absent-minded professor. Thomson slipped onto the floor, bleating and holding his side. McHenry lurched back, tipping his chair and cackling, a hand wiping sweat from his forehead. Others, who had known Carton as long as I had, were genuinely touched and slapped me on the shoulder and back. Even Carton was swept up in this sentimental hysteria. I saw him dabbing tears in his eyes, saying, "Yes, yes. I remember!"

I walked to the table where the maitre d' had hidden leftover rolls from the meal. Like a shadow, McHenry was at my side. He called to the maitre d', "Say, Gene. Any of that great salmon left?" I buttered a roll and the maitre d' stomped off to the kitchen. (Half an hour earlier he'd made his last call for food.)

"Great story," McHenry said to me. "When I take over, Carton is out."

"But he's retiring in three years," I said weakly.

"He'll be happy to retire early to his farm. But don't worry, you're safe—"

"Boys boys boys," Thomson shouted in our ears, grabbing our shoulders to steady himself. "What have you two been conspiring about?" McHenry suddenly gagged on something and dashed to the bathroom. "Professor," Thomson whispered to me, but in a whisper the whole room could hear, "I want to say what a lovely lovely lovely story . . . like being back in the old days, that was a great house we had there, the golf course in my back yard, a nightcap at Sal's on Lake Calhoun . . . Where was I?"

"Minneapolis," someone said, laughing.

"Yes. But Carton—where is that rascal?—oh here you are. You remember the time you began fumigating the silo in New Prague with three men still inside it, and then somehow you managed to blame them so I had to fire the lot? I can't remember what it was you did well—but we loved you just the same."

"Here, here," several voices said, choked with real emotion, glasses raised. Carton's face showed an amazing mixture of fear, joy, and self-pity. But Thomson had twisted facts. In a rare on-site visit, he had rushed the fumigation. Carton graciously took the blame for the near disaster.

I escaped the stuffy room again well after four. I turned off the floodlights myself when I saw the strands of light washing over the river. I took a big company grain sack and my hand shovel, and walked along the shore behind the restaurant. Steam rose from the water and mingled with trails of fog. To the east one could begin to discern the ribs of the Mercier Bridge jutting out above the eddies of white mist. I found a spot to dig—twisted dry reeds and river garbage. I liked to overturn this sort of debris, which was rich with life, and let the insects rouse themselves a bit before choosing my samples, so it took me a few minutes to prepare the earth. McHenry must have watched me on my knees troweling, as if in a garden, with no apparent purpose other than to turn over dirt. His sharp voice piercing the river rush of sounds made my heart skip. "What the hell are you doing?" he asked.

I stood up, waving my shovel at him. "Get away," I said.

He backed off and his eyes widened. "I'll just stand over here out of your way," he said, suddenly timid.

"No," I said. "I've had enough of you."

He stooped to pick up the grain sack with the company logo on it, obviously to engage in some activity other than being glared at by me. "Are you allowed to take these?"

"Of course I am."

"I'm sorry," he said. "I'll go." But he didn't. "I was only curious," he said. "You're a famous character with that crew inside. Everyone likes you, everyone *admires* you, but you're a bloody cereal chemist. You have less power than the most out-of-the-way grain elevator foreman."

"I can see why you're curious," I said. "You have power and no one likes you."

"Yes, yes," he said enthusiastically, as if I had not just insulted him. "But what I'm really curious about is this respect you have. Colleagues and friends in other firms respect my work and efficiency, they admire the *job* I've done straightening this company out. And let me tell you it's been quite a job. But no one admires me. I am only as admirable as my work, and people forget a job well done a month later."

"Perhaps you're simply not an admirable man," I said.

"Yes, that could be," he said, thoughtfully raking his sweat-spiked hair with one hand. Now I noticed the stream of perspiration down his temples and neck, the tight collar of his shirt soaking wet. He still wore his tie. McHenry's legs buckled, but he caught himself and said in a high-pitched voice, "One of my boys is a botanist at the University of Michigan. Very young to be a professor." A puzzled look crossed his face, and I remembered Carton's gossip about McHenry's children. I reached out to give him a hand, but he said, "No! No, don't. This was on the farm. Winnie and Max just about at the end of their rope raising mink and chinchilla"—I had no idea whom he was talking about, or what; his face had turned white—"and this cousin from Winnipeg comes for the summer. He was tall like me but couldn't ride a horse, couldn't shoot a gun, wouldn't go into town with us to yell at the whores, know what I mean?" I nodded. "All he did was walk in the woods, writing things down in a blasted little notebook. Alice protected him, so what could I do, and he hid that notebook, damned if I could find it, or he always had it with him. But one day, two days before he was to leave, Alice and Winnie made him teach them the new dances and I found the notebook under his pillow—I read it in one of the fox barns—I nearly cried—he'd never set foot in our forest, but here he was describing things, understanding them, better than he had a right to. He knew those woods better in the first week than I did in fourteen years. It was all written down!"

I looked away for a moment at the morning star on

the horizon, and when I glanced at McHenry again, he had fallen on his face into the soft pile of my debris. I knelt to undo his tie, but he crawled away from me. The back door to the restaurant slammed and I heard garbage cans being knocked over, car doors banging, boyish screams, and Thomson shouting, "Professor, Professor, where are you?" As they rounded the corner of the building, they saw me. I was standing over the fallen figure of McHenry, which amused them. "Fight! Fight! Who won?" They came running and skipping toward us. Between the restaurant and this section of shore was a small muddy bog. I had no desire to warn them of its deceptive nature—it appeared solid enough to walk on. Five of them fell right into it, also on their faces. An act of sheer theatrics: there was an instant when I could see Thomson physically decide to fall, with a giddy shout, rather than veer off to the left. Carton and three others managed to stop just on the brink, Carton's arms flying out to prevent them from falling. A moment of silence followed. Then Thomson lifted himself partly out of the muck. "Oh, Professor." He laughed. "Help us evolve back into human beings."

I had the maitre d' spray the mud off the men with his powerful hose. They stood in the jet of water, heads bowed, no longer laughing, hangovers catching up with them. Carton drove the out-of-town execu-

tives to their hotel downtown. I drove three of the
locals to their nearby homes. I watched carefully as
each of my soggy charges weaved over well-groomed
lawns to their nearly identical Tudor homes. I returned to the restaurant at five because I'd forgotten
my shovel on the riverbank. McHenry still lay where
I'd left him, half awake, but with dirt-caked hands.
My grain sack was full to the bursting. "Is that what
you wanted?" he asked, pointing a muddy finger at
the debris and then the bag. He had filled it with his
bare hands. (The shovel lay just a yard away, behind
him.) I thanked him for his trouble. But he seemed
quite comfortable where he lay, so I took the grain
sack and shovel, and said goodbye.

*Reared from white grublike larvae in burrows in soft
rotting logs. Larvae collected in November and held
in poly bag in unheated garage over winter. Larvae
pupated in early April following year and adult*
Trichiotini *emerged on dates shown on locality
label. Roxboro, Quebec. May 5, 1967.*

Now that I'm retired I view time in larger blocks, but
the days seem shorter. After a church deacons' meeting today—on a Monday morning!—I drove to my

supply store in Mount Royal for the two chemicals that, as ingredients in a new recipe for poison, prevent the gumming of wings. Then I stopped by the Expo site to watch construction and check for any recently upturned earth—many finds. Then I crossed the river to the Lac St. Louis swamp, and before I knew it the sun was setting. When my wife saw the mud caked up to the hips of my pants, she burst into tears. The transition, from my working to not working, is more difficult for her; she expects me to be home all day, but when I am, I'm always in her way. The *Trichiotini* in the garage amazed me—must write old Beetle Brow in Ottawa to tell him of my small discovery. He used to think the stages were of stop-and-go growth, then sudden transformation. I can prove my point. Most of the cellular reorganization occurs in the first week of pupation. I am able with this new freedom to spend hours in utter concentration. In the swamp today I stumbled over a paper wasps' nest, but by standing still for several minutes I avoided a bad case of stings. I am practically immune, anyway. One landed upon my raised hand on the flesh between thumb and forefinger. The husky abdomen twitched back and forth. He was a handsome creature: black fringed by yellow that banded the solid brown body. Unlike cricket hunters or mud daubers, he appeared solid enough to withstand a strong wind. He stood as still as I was the instant before inserting his stinger.

The filament of fiber, in certain of these insects strong and flexible enough to penetrate oak, seemed to corkscrew into my skin, then slipped out. I don't know why. He left no poison and when he flew off all the rest did, too, and I resumed my business.

Of the family Pantatomidae, *three variations, all similar to* Murgantia histrionica, Harlequin Cabbage Bug. *Their collector, H. J. Farmer, estimated the field they were collected in was three acres and held two to three million bugs. Westerly winds. Dry soil and vegetation. Common annual event around the lake, according to the locals. Tihany, by Lake Balaton, Hungary. October 1, 1969.*

"It's snowing," one of my grandsons had said when we drove up to the Hotel Moderne in Tihany. But it was a hot fall night, so we paid little attention to the swirling mists around all the outdoor lamps until my son's wife pulled back the bed sheets for her children. They found eight stink bugs digging into the folds, and I was called in for an inspection. We examined the windows and hallways, and found dozens more. My grandsons, Stephen and Humphrey, ran outside and returned breathless. "They've coated the building. Millions of them," Stephen said. Humphrey said, "They seem to swarm around the lights," and he sensibly suggested that we turn off the bedroom lights if we didn't want any more. My wife spoke in a whisper about the insects, staring at me as if I were responsible for them. My son's wife said, "I'm going to have a talk with the manager about this." But my son, who is on sabbatical leave from his college for a year, teased her. "You should have a talk with the stink bugs." Then he laughed. "This is the resort spot of all of Eastern Europe?"

Well after midnight, I met Stephen on my way to the bathroom in the hall. "They're not very noisy," he said, "but I think I hear them crawling through the cracks in the windows. Squeeak, they go. I can't sleep." I couldn't either, because of an ache in my legs that reminded me of what adults called growing pains when I was a teenager. We sat up for a while in the lobby and let the bearded desk clerk regale us, as far as we could tell, with tales about giant insects and flying saucers. He was hunched behind his bureau, over a small lamp, and, despite the shadows that danced around the room, he seemed barely to move. He spoke no English, but by the time we bowed to say good night, the big man was our fast friend.

The next morning Stephen asked, "What are we looking for?"

"The center of the swarm, if there is one," Humphrey said. "These insects don't normally gather like this. We are fascinated by the possibility of discovering an entirely new pattern of social behavior."

I did not want to contradict him—the Asian Stink Bug apparently did migrate up the Danube plain from the Black Sea in the early fall, although the desk clerk seemed to say it had not happened for several years—but Humphrey sounded so sure of himself, whether he told facts or his own fantasy facts. He called himself the "other entomologist of the family." He was very happy with these stink bugs, which are closely related to leaf hoppers. He had chosen to collect these insects and true bugs in order not to compete with me—I collect beetles. He was saying, "We want to observe this behavior close up, watch for a central structure. Most swarming insects follow a group of leaders."

"I observed their behavior last night," Stephen said. "I smelled enough." He made pig sounds.

"Quiet," Humphrey said. "Do you want a billion bugs descending on you?"

I turned away to untangle my net from barbed wire and saw a swallow zigzag over the next field. Several other swallows dipped below the tree line, then wheeled off along the horizon. These birds often nest in cliffs like the short limestone bluffs I had seen along the lake. The stink bugs may have been destroying their nests. I heard a sharp grunt and turned to find my grandsons wrestling on the ground. They were fighting over me. Earlier, Stephen had tried to convince us to go rowing on the lake, where there wasn't "so much to talk about." But Humphrey had a morbid fear of water. I spoke the boys' names and their battle stopped instantly.

Stephen and I were resting next to a windbreak of poplars that separated two writhing fields of the insects. My grandson held my hand in a painful grip, so we knelt down and stood up in unison, trading killing bottle and aspirator. We peered together into my net, which caught hundreds of the bugs. Stephen normally dreaded this last activity for fear of finding wasps. Humphrey had strayed into one field, prancing like a cat in snow, raising small storms of stink bugs wherever he moved. Then, at another end of the field, a great cloud of the bugs flew into the air. The noise was like a stampede of cattle. The pink sky turned brown. Stephen ducked behind me and hid his face in my ribs. When the stink bugs landed, the instant of quiet was as awesome as the massive sound they made.

Something in the tree above us whistled. The desk clerk had wedged himself between the Y limbs of a poplar. My grandson stepped away from me and shouted, "What do you think you're doing up in that tree? Can't you see there are *billions* of bugs here?"

The desk clerk tipped an imaginary cap and pointed to a small cottage on the far corner of the field, opposite us. A curl of smoke rose from its chimney. He began to talk calmly, the same reassuring gibberish as the night before. Then he let out a shriek and flapped his arms—a black swarm of stink bugs had landed on the cottage—and a whole section of the field Humphrey was in flew off the ground. Stephen said, "My brother!" ripping free of my hand as he ran off. The desk clerk fell to the earth with a thud, not more than a foot from me.

The desk clerk gestured for me to give him a hand standing up. I did so without asking how he felt—it was beyond my sign language. For a moment we both watched the young boy, who had reached the spot in the field where Humphrey had fallen. Like a magician, Stephen pulled his brother out of the tall grass. The next instant they were fighting. The desk clerk tapped me on the arm, bowed, said something in a gracious tone, then limped off in the boys' direction. When he arrived, my grandsons picked themselves off the ground and beat the dust out of their pants like little cowboys. There was a strange lull in the insect noise. The desk clerk took Stephen by the hand, which my grandson responded to by bowing slightly, mimicking the Hungarian. But the desk clerk suddenly slapped the boy's bottom. Even fifty yards away I heard the sound. He turned to Humphrey, who obediently raised his hand. Thwack. For a moment afterward the desk clerk appeared to lecture them, then ran off to his cabin.

When I arrived I had to laugh, even though the boys were sobbing like six-year-olds. "What did he say?" I asked. Stephen gulped angrily and said, "You *know,* Grampa. His English doesn't work." Humphrey burst out laughing, but at the same moment the stink bugs dropped from the sky in a feeding frenzy. Prickly parts of them stuck to our skin. They flew into our mouths. Wings beat furiously against our ears. I shouted, "To the lake, boys!"

We fell into the muddy mouth of a stream. We were screaming with joy and terror as we plucked the bugs off one another. The last one desperately evaded my fingers in Stephen's thick hair, seeming to dig into the scalp; then suddenly it flew as if obeying a command, with thousands of others around us, and millions in the field we'd fled from. The stench of squashed stink bugs hung in the air, a brown mist. We crawled ashore and lay on our backs, too tired to laugh now, but heroes of our own small adventures.

Sifting badly rotten logs lying in an open field. The soft, punky heartwood was crumbling before my sifting. The logs had been in this location some ten years. Roxboro, Quebec. September 20, 1970.

"I used to make so many recipes from memory," Ettie said, upstairs. "Oh dear me no, you too?" She was either on the phone or talking with our neighbor Bonnie, whose voice was inaudible until she laughed. The only light down here in the basement, other than my microscope lamp, came from the laundry room. When I had retrieved the petri dishes of *Collembola* from the spare fridge, I'd flicked on the light switch above the dryer. I preferred complete darkness; the contrasts were stronger. I froze these beetles so that I could examine them longer under the hot light. The tiny droplets of condensation would vanish, evaporating—they seemed to explode into nothingness. I was haphazardly looking for an undamaged specimen.

The codeine for my back spasms made it feel like evening—I wasn't sure exactly what time it was. Groggy movements, mechanical sighting through the microscope lens. But Ettie spoke from the kitchen in her midafternoon tone of voice: "I said to her . . . a bath every night in Epsom . . . Oh not kidney . . . yes, her daughter poor thing finally married . . ." Then the neighbor on the other side, Irina, howled at her Doberman pinscher, "Yi, yi, yi, Sasha," and our other neighbor Bonnie, evidently in the kitchen too, laughed. "The mad Russian is still alive, bless her soul."

"That awful woman," Ettie said, and I knew it was nearly three o'clock, the afternoon feeding for Sasha.

When a familiar smell wafted up at me I followed it, perhaps instinctively imitating Sasha, who often rooted about in our garden. Accustomed to the bright light under the microscope, my eyes were momentarily baffled by the relative darkness they met. The aroma was of old books my mother laid on my lap as she read them to me over my shoulder. Or the Canada balsam turpentine we used in the Calgary lab for curing cutaway views of grain on microscope slides. The voices upstairs were no longer intelligible, only bird sounds. My mother read me a naturalist's book, *Bears I Have Known in Manitoba,* by a man I later learned had never left his campus office in Winnipeg to write the book. Then I saw what I was smelling: a flat green tin for chewing tobacco. An entomologist I met once in Arizona had mailed it from Mexico— poison, a new recipe. I used to make so many from memory. How long had I been inhaling it? Why had I left its top off? Absent-minded from the codeine.

I stood and fell onto one of the spare beds by my work table in a simple, unified motion. Bonnie's friendly voice pierced the heavy air of the basement. "Elwyn, dear man, what are you doing down there?" I lay on the bed for a long time, considering the question. Did she mean what did I normally do down here, making boxes, examining, treating, and mounting beetles, transferring the necessary information about each insect to a tiny notecard I pinned underneath it? Or did she mean what was I doing falling down on a bed?

A loud scratching directly overhead delayed my reply. I sat up and saw the muzzle of the dog trying to dig in the well of the basement window. Cha cha cha, it went. Or Sasha, Sasha. Ettie's voice boomed, startlingly near me because of the shape of the basement stairway: a square bell. "I don't care if your husband did die in a plane crash," she yelled at Irina through the screen door—I could hear even the whistle the screen caused in Ettie's voice. "You keep that dog in your yard or I'll call the police." I was helpless to the logic of my wife's threat. The dog *was* Irina's husband. She had renamed it after him when her husband was killed. It had been just a puppy three years ago when news of the plane crash arrived. Its great spurt of growth Dobermans are famous for occurred in the following month, when Irina went crazy with grief.

Ripples of shadow formed halos around the opaque window where the dog's head bobbed. Sasha stopped, jerked back by its owner, but for a moment I was aware of something other than Sasha's head still disturbing the air and light of the basement well window. When the light and sounds of normalcy returned, I realized I had been hallucinating. The Mexican poison may have been the cause. My jaw ached. Was I in danger? Probably not—I remembered the ingredients the entomologist from Arizona had written in his letter with the package. I remembered a story he told of being bitten by a rattlesnake while collecting. He was relatively sure the venom would not be fatal. He drove home and took notes of each new stage of the sensation. He called his doctor only after recovering his senses, and he published the notes in an article for *Scientific American*. He'd written about waves of clarity and dementia. "Elwyn Farmer," Bonnie called. "We've got a neighborhood crisis on our hands."

The light of day was unbearable. The kitchen was flooded with such intense sunlight I could not see. Needles of panic rolled over me. "Elwyn?" Bonnie said somewhere. She was such a good soul. She was off to my right, likely seated in the chair next to the phone she enjoyed answering for Ettie—to gossip with my wife's friends. "Elwyn, what's the matter?" I told her I couldn't see, and she burst out laughing. "Of course you can't. Your eyes are closed." The involuntary mechanism of eyelids squinting suddenly stopped. "Your wife is cultivating her garden and local international relations," Bonnie said. Irina was throwing leaves over one side of the hedge that separated our yards. On the other side my wife was throwing them back. I touched the handle of the

screen door and the leaves flying in the air became
locusts. Irina saw me and began to swear. Words I
knew well from the office, which gradually lost their
meaning so that the woman with the red face and pile
of hair on top of her head seemed to be singing in her
native tongue, Lithuanian. I saw Bonnie's face next to
mine, immense sadness spreading across her freckles.
"Hello, Irina," Bonnie said. The swearing stopped
because Irina had not yet "excommunicated" Bonnie.
"Who would name their dog after her dead husband?" Bonnie whispered to me.

"Mind you, she's had a hard life," Ettie said over her
tea. My hand gripped my jaw, which I hoped wasn't
obvious. My pulse rate was twice as fast as normal.
"Her poor husband," said Bonnie, who was spinning
the lazy Susan. "The Russian concentration camps
they were in. Separated, reunited in Sweden."

"Or was it Norway?" Ettie asked. "Her husband
was such a fine man. He drove all the neighbor children to school over in Westmount every day when the
English school closed over at Dollard. But she domi-
nated him."

"He spoiled her," Bonnie said. "Have you ever
eaten her food? She never had to cook—he did all the
cooking."

They both laughed, and the refrigerator pump
starting up made me jump. I noticed my wife's silver
hair was thinning—pink patches of skull showed.

Bonnie's left hand had an oblong brown spot she picked at unconsciously. Ettie had been furious with me moments before, a rage of embarrassment, but now her knee knocked against mine, inanimate love. I could see straight ahead but not up or down—my eyes were locked. As long as I sat still, the racing heart was not too painful. But I could not talk or make more than a few words stand up in a row against one another. The infinite possibilities of sentence and phrase crippled my tongue. Bonnie and Ettie did not seem to notice the symptoms of this Mexican hallucinogen that also killed beetles, which I had accidentally inhaled.

"Mind you, I worry," my wife said. "She may come at us with an ax one day."

"Oh honey, she's a harmless old thing," Bonnie said.

"Her bark is worse," I said, thinking I'd completed but feeling the palpable incompleteness of the thought.

"Oh hush, Elwyn, you should talk," Ettie said.

Bonnie took my hand. "Our Elwyn wouldn't harm a flea—of course, tell that to all the miles of beetles stuck on pins downstairs."

"Honestly," Ettie said, "sometimes I just don't know what to do with him."

Northampton, Massachusetts
December 1973

I sat on my borrowed bed, partials in their glass, pajamas still under the pillow, T-shirt on. One grandson in the adjoining room was writing an essay for
a high school English class. The door to Stephen's
bedroom was shut. I could hear the boy thinking.
Quiet cries of exasperation every few minutes. An
occasional hand slapped the desk and rattled pens
in their coffee can. The flexible lamp creaked like
human bones. I had only two means of escape: the
door to Stephen's room and a door that opened onto
the attic stairs.

At the turn of the century, the attic was the ser-
vants' quarters. My wife and I used to stay up there in
the only furnished room when we visited. But our
other grandson, Humphrey, had taken over the space.
He was home from college now, entertaining friends
in the suite of attic rooms. The nearly imperceptible
clink of billiard balls drifted by my ears. Incense
burned. Two boys and Humphrey had trundled up
the stairs a few minutes ago, stopping to inquire why
I was reading a book called *Three Men in a Boat*.
"Because we took a trip on the same stretch of the
Thames in England," Humphrey had explained effi-
ciently for his grandfather, although that was not at
all the reason. It had seemed the other way around.
The trip was made catering to my favorite book. But

these teenagers said, "Hey, great," the words dripping out like syrup.

My wife was asleep in her granddaughter's room. Our granddaughter slept in the study. We were an inconvenience to this family now. Once we had been almost indispensable.

Other noises came from the family room downstairs, where my son and daughter-in-law sat watching television. I found myself laughing along whenever my son did, infected by what he found funny even at this distance.

Stephen burst out of his bedroom and shouted down the back stairs, "Will you quit having so much fun with the television. I'm in agony."

The family room door opened and Henry arrived at the foot of the stairs. He laughed up, quoting something from *King Lear,* which Stephen was writing his essay about. Stephen hissed and rushed back into his room, slamming the door. I came out of hiding and saw Henry in an odd posture, head cocked to one side, but a smile frozen on his face. "Do you want me to interfere?" I asked.

"No, no. The poor boy needs to be left alone."

Henry returned to the family room, gently closing the door, and immediately barked at something on the television. The bark was followed by a series of high-rolling vowels.

After a hesitant knock, I asked, "Stephen?"

"What," the boy said in a flat voice. "Who is it?

Go away." He opened the door. "Oh Elwyn, it's you."

We stood for a moment, staring directly into each other's eyes—Stephen's displayed a frightening lack of focus. Then he growled, "I'm in an ugly mood," and shuffled to his desk in slippers worn away at the heels. Something to buy him for Christmas, I noted. The boy turned over every sheet of paper on the desk so that the sides with writing lay face down. When Stephen saw how obvious this gesture had been, he went red and dropped with a thud into his chair. His huge bush of hair rustled over his shoulders. "I was just thinking about your essay," I said. But I had been doing no such thing. I only wanted the boy's company when it was plain Stephen least needed an old fool puttering around his room. My thoughts panicked. I tried to remember something, anything, about *King Lear*. "We call it a paper nowadays, Grampa," Stephen said. "Essay is kind of an old-fashioned word. Besides, that makes it sound even harder to do."

I knew I should leave. The shoulders of my grandson vibrated as he fussed with pens, paper, books on his desk; as he pushed the typewriter back an inch, then pulled it forward a fraction of an inch. But an invisible force held me in the room—not simply the inertia of love or age. In my old age, my precarious sense of stability seemed to depend on understanding children at their own level, which I could never do when I was a younger man, when my own two sons were underfoot.

"Let me see . . . Lear," I said.

Stephen stood up and said, "Grampa."

But I could not stop myself. "If I remember correctly," I said, "There are three little girls and a question of who loves Grampa Lear most."

Stephen slumped onto his cluttered couch. "Elwyn," he said, but undisguised tenderness now trembled in his voice. (Stephen had not been listening, however, his glance jerking from fingernails to the bright orange pen stuck between couch cushions to the tip of his shirt collar darkened by flipping between his thumb and forefinger thousands of times.) "I don't know why I'm kidding myself," Stephen said. "My father teaches philosophy, but I haven't got a thought in my brain. I'm not even sure I have a brain." Stephen giggled, and out of relief I joined him with a chuckle, clutching the bed below to make sure it lay where I expected to sit. But Stephen took offense at some deeply personal, self-inflicted insult and snapped his fingers savagely, which arrested me halfway down to the bed. "I am serious," he said. "You all think. I know you do. Humphrey thinks and talks at the same time. It's amazing. I've seen him do it every day of my life, even under pressure at debate tournaments. Just like that, words gush out which show he has already thought out at least a few of the ideas he spouts. In arguments, he just demolishes anyone—like me—who is hearing his own words for the first time when they tumble out. Dad thinks without talking, but you can tell he's been thinking about you and actually planned a whole elaborate response to something you said weeks ago."

Stephen took a breath, and I was caught thinking myself, losing my chance to interject kind, reassuring words. "And you, Grampa," Stephen continued, "you can tell these long elaborate stories about your life or about science and beetles, and you always have a point in mind—I may get lost sometimes, just drift pleasantly along with your voice, but at the end—every time—there it is. A reason for telling the story. A point. A punchline. I can't do any of that. I look inside myself when I'm talking—like right now—and all I see are words. This is unusual, you know, me talking. Most of the time I want to say something and the words just aren't there, like a comic strip character before the words are put in the balloon. I get this dumb look. My friends stare at me, their lips curling to the left, unconsciously imitating the way I talk out of the side of my mouth—"

"Grampa," Henry said on the stairs, "you're not bothering Stephen, are you?" Stephen stood up again, changed in an instant to the sullenly silent boy he was moments before. He returned to his desk chair and fell into it, back to his audience.

"Grampa," Henry said, "I think we should leave Stephen alone." But he stayed on the threshold of the door. The house settled along several of its fault lines. "So, how's it coming?" he asked Stephen, who groaned. "Did you think about limiting the topic to Edmund, say, or Edgar? You liked those characters—"

Stephen swiveled around in his chair, a rush of words coming out. "I can think all I want. Whatever I write comes out no more than a page long. I need *five* pages. Can't you write the damn thing for me?"

"I'd flunk if I wrote it." Henry laughed.

"Don't say that!" Stephen shrieked. "If you flunk, how can I conceivably pass?"

"Look, Stephen," Henry said, his lips hardening. "How many times have you read the play?"

"Once," Stephen whispered.

"That's not enough."

"I get hives when I read too much," Stephen said. Tears came to his eyes. "I can't do it again."

"You don't have to read the whole thing, damn it," Henry said. "Only the parts you're writing about."

"All right!" Stephen shouted. He jumped to his feet. "Party's over. Everybody out, out, out."

I climbed the attic stairs, putting my full weight on each creak. But no one seemed to hear me. I walked boldly down the hall. The door to the unfurnished room was open a crack. Low murmurs drifted out. Billiard balls clicked into one another. Across from the poolroom was the bedroom, and at the end of the hall behind this cluster of doorways was a large walk-in closet, where my eldest grandson Humphrey kept his collection of insects.

When we arrived this afternoon, Humphrey took me aside and said solemnly, "I dropped out of my biology course this semester. There were too many premeds. I've decided to major in French." This news contained a few phrases in code that I asked my grandson to decipher: "drop out" and "premed." Once they were explained, I began to realize what Humphrey meant. Despite his extraordinary gifts in the field, the budding entomologist was not going to become an academic entomologist. "Of course I'll always love it as a hobby," Humphrey said. "I'll never be completely cured of it."

I wandered into the walk-in closet, where a single light was burning. I sat down for a moment to examine my grandson's progress. A voice broke the silence, from the intercom Henry installed to avoid shouting up two flights of stairs. "Boys," Henry said over the intercom. "Maybe it's time to come downstairs and smoke your marijuana in the living room. You remember our agreement about fire safety?"

Someone rushed across the hall into the bedroom, shutting my closet door as he passed it. "Dad," Humphrey said, "we're not smoking tonight. But the general consensus here is that you are the most liberal parents in the Valley."

You can be heard from downstairs only by pressing the "talk" button, which Henry did simply to laugh at this light sarcasm. There was a pause. "Well, anyway," Henry said, "come down for a drink when you've finished not smoking." Humphrey laughed and ran back to the poolroom.

The boys giggled. The sound of someone inhaling deeply rose over the subsiding giggles. "All right, now put it out," Humphrey said. "Not on the pool table, you idiot."

The game resumed, a click here, a thud there. No talk. It was obvious they were smoking marijuana, which did not bother me. I myself felt a little "stoned," according to my grandson's description of the sensation: slowed down, happy to examine the minutiae of the natural world, as if my eyes had become capable of microscopic vision. Come to think of it, this state of mind was familiar. I often went into a sort of trance when I was out collecting, or even as I worked in my basement, mounting, labeling, sifting, building boxes.

Several summers ago Humphrey admitted he smoked marijuana. "It's the only time I don't feel such a tremendous urge to talk, when I smoke it," he told me. "I know I talk too much in real life. People think you're more intelligent when you're silent. I've heard that said about Stephen. I don't bother to dispel the misconception." Humphrey laughed and I asked if that was how he really felt about his brother. "Of course not," he said. "Stephen's very sweet—for a severely retarded child."

I found myself calmly reading the locality notes my grandson wrote so well. I let my eyes drift over a work table that represented my own deep influence on this boy and Humphrey's delightful innovations on the techniques it took me thirty years to achieve. I turned off the microscope lamp, and in the darkness the smell of mothballs became overpowering. I wondered whether I had noticed the smell before, or if odors intensified in the dark. It was time to reveal myself to my neighbors.

My knock on the door sent footfalls stomping around the room.

"Grampa," Humphrey said. "We didn't hear you come up the stairs."

"Hello, Mr. Farmer," two voices said from the shadows.

"I'm sorry to disturb your game," I said. "I couldn't sleep."

"We weren't making too much noise, were we?" one of the boys asked. He stepped up to the table and into the light and casually laid his hand over its false-wood rim, covering a hand-rolled cigarette I would not have noticed had the boy not tried to hide it. He had long straight hair and a flat, uninflected way of speaking.

"Not at all," I said. "At my age sleep becomes a little redundant. What are your names again?"

"Peter," said the boy with the long hair.

The other said, "John," morosely. John's hair was short, out of the fashion, and already thinning on top. He was Humphrey's age but appeared much older, a bank teller who had wandered into the wrong house.

"Would you like to play?" Peter asked. "I just racked up."

"You'll have to refresh my memory on the rules; it's been years since—"

"Elwyn knows how to play," Humphrey said, laughing meanly. "He was table tennis champion of all Alberta in 1936. He's playing dumb; it's the old pool shark coming out in him."

"Need I remind you, Humphrey," John said roundly, "that table tennis is akin to pool only in that it is played indoors on green tables?"

Peter explained the rules to me, but in such a bored, unhappy way I had to ask if he wanted to play with someone else.

"No," he said from behind hair that formed a curtain when he leaned over the table. "I'll break."

For a few minutes, we played in silence. Peter cursed when he missed shots, but his voice conveyed the same hostile boredom even in his curses. John and Humphrey sat at each end of the old couch and chuckled from time to time for no obvious reason. My eyes slowly adjusted to the smoky light. Before

the pool table was installed—only a few months ago
—this room had been a large storage area, which
snaked under tight ceiling-to-floor eaves from one
end of the house to the other. Old children's toys and
games were stored here, books, outgrown clothes,
abandoned coin, stamp, and now insect collections,
discarded furniture. A square window at the base of
one corner opened like a small door onto the flat roof
of the upstairs porch, where the children were sometimes sent to fix the television aerial—another child
on the front lawn shouting relayed instructions from
the family room. With the addition of the pool table,
the storage area had simply been pushed back so that
metal shelves stood side to side, front to back, and
piles of boxes teetered on top of one another. I remembered now that these rooms had always stirred
fear in the children, even the usually fearless Humphrey. Wasps built nests outside in the eaves, tunneled
into the wood, and occasionally found themselves
confused and doomed in a dark, hot, dusty interior.

We heard a creak on the stairs, and all became alert.
Peter, who had been lining up a shot, stood straight
and put a finger to his lips. Humphrey and John
froze, both holding old *National Geographic*s in awkward positions away from their bodies. I laughed. "I
don't seem to walk importantly enough. You didn't
hear *me* coming up the stairs."

The three boys spoke with one voice. "Hey, yeah,"

and Peter elaborated: "We're not *doing* anything. Your grandfather's here."

I did not like being referred to in the third person.

The next moment, when Stephen cautiously entered the room, it was as if the boys had never broken out of the poses they'd been in before the creak of the stairs. I was the only one to greet my second grandson.

"Can I play?" he timidly asked Peter, who continued to line up his shot without looking at Stephen.

"Elwyn and I are playing."

I told Stephen he could step in for me, but Peter said, "No. I'm winning."

"We were just going out for a walk, anyway," Humphrey said as he stood up and stretched.

John said, "This is the first I've heard of a walk. Oh, that's right." He saw Peter flash something in his open palm. "Now I remember. We're going for a walk by Paradise Pond."

"It's fifteen degrees out," Stephen said.

Stephen and I convinced the three grumpy boys to let us join them on their walk. "It defeats the purpose of taking a walk," Peter said, but Humphrey had a change of heart. We passed through the television room, where questions were asked about other parents as our winter coats were pulled on. John and I wore the same kind of galoshes. "No traction," I said. "But I like the way they squeak," he said.

In the outdoors we forgot our minor animosities and remembered how beautiful it could be on a cold moonlit night. "No bugs to collect," Stephen said. I said I could rustle up a few if necessary. Humphrey and Stephen walked on ahead, talking quietly, something I had not seen them do in many years. Peter and John asked me about beetles, pygmy rattlesnakes they claimed I'd been bitten by, the Gulf Coast of Florida, where my wife and I were heading after Christmas.

By the pond on the college campus, the wind picked up. Snow drifted across the path we took away from the pond. It appeared to be snowing, but it was only this drifting. I told stories about dust storms during the Depression, how some farmers dug huge trenches to prevent the soil from blowing away.

The moon gave off plenty of light, but in a small clearing where the river bent Peter stopped and lit a match. He put a partly smoked cigarette to his lips and inhaled deeply. "I hope you don't mind, Mr. Farmer," he said.

"Not at all," I said.

"It's marijuana," Stephen said.

Humphrey and John gathered around Peter and solemnly studied the orange glow of the cigarette. Stephen turned his back on this scene, pretending to look up the trackless path. The odor of the marijuana, which struck my senses so quickly in this cold air, caused me to think of a hot August day in a southern

he sank up to his ankles in the muck, but he quickly learned the gentle tread necessary for walking on such soft earth. When he arrived, he said nothing. He thrust his hands in his pockets and followed one yard behind me, stooping over the net whenever I did, but stepping back whenever I showed him the insides of it. But when he saw my growing frustration with the dew, he put a finger on the extra nets that I carried under one arm. He took the longer one, unscrewed the neck, and began to beat the grass in front of me with the wooden pole. He pointed to a spot just above the grass level that he meant me to sweep. I was looking for a dew-drinking beetle that was happiest in this weather after a day of thundershowers. I applauded the boy's ingenuity, but I played it close to the chest, as he did. Because of his short pants I decided he was French. He was no more than ten years old. Soon his friends arrived and were instructed with amazingly few words (by means of ear-kissing whispers) to find long sticks and imitate him. I followed behind a fan of half a dozen silent children beating a field for me. I never found the beetle, but when a pregnant ichneumon fly emerged from my net, singing her tiny song, I gathered the boys around me. They huddled like football players. I asked them if they spoke English. The first one nodded, but he had not yet spoken a word to me. I explained how these insects plant their eggs in other insects' young. The larvae that emerge eat whatever living tissue they encounter. I said this particular mother, if she can't find a suitable host, will have to eject her eggs before they begin devouring her. The boy translated. His friends did not understand. He illustrated the idea with one hand spread flat and made a *brat brat brat* sound, like a machine gun. His friends laughed, slapping each other on the back, and mimicked his dive-bombing plane. When an oceangoing ship passed near the shore, they dispersed. But the one boy remained, staring at his muddy shoes. The red and white hull of the big boat, as a backdrop through the trees, dwarfed him for a moment. Finally he just looked up at the sky and walked away.

Sifting dense mats of short grass along a ditch in woodland dried pond. Squares of grass mats cut out with saw and torn apart as sifted. Material damp. Pond and ditch had water within last two months. Destin, Florida. February 1980.

Drought in this balmy climate sears the earth, as if a swarm of hover jets from the air force base across the bay had hung over every square inch of ground. Because the soil is saturated with water so much of the year, it dries out quickly. Normally resistant to the worst natural and man-made disasters, insect life is devastated. I find termite nests in chaos, ants eating one another. But my beetles happened to live in a rare patch of wet earth. Cutting into their thriving community made me think of Canada before the dust bowl of the thirties. Now the sun will bake them into hysteria, like all the rest of us. Two feet below them is the spongy water table. We are less than a mile from the Gulf of Mexico. My fourteen-year-old granddaughter, Greg's girl, seated on a hillock above me, asked why they don't just dig down to the water, if it's there. "They don't know it's there," I said, thinking about my own grandparents, who settled on a flood plain by the Green River in Ontario because of its fertile soil. After five years of flooding, they abandoned the land and the only two-story house in the district.

"But what about those beetles that tell time?" my granddaughter asked.

"That's instinct," I said. "Not knowledge. An ant out on the prowl for food seems to recognize another ant from its colony, but closer inspection shows the ant only reacts to a familiar odor. Wash off the ant and place him in his own colony, and he'll be attacked. Humans think, insects act on tropic responses." But I remembered my father, who at forty insisted the only way to cure his bursitis was to sleep on the soft clay banks of the Bow River. One night he was swept downriver by a flash flood. He claimed he awoke the next morning seven miles from where he'd started, dry, beached on an almost identical bank.

"But how does that beetle know what time it is?" my granddaughter asked.

I tried to concentrate on the question. "It doesn't know," I said. "We don't know. It may be a mystery."

"But when you told me the story before, you knew," she said.

"Well, I forgot. You tell me."

Her face wrinkled. She stood up and smoothed out her dress and came down to my side. She took my hand and started to lead me home. "You said it had nothing to do with the darkness," she said. "Your friend thought it was the darkness, but another friend said it was the way ferns folded up at night. Now do you remember?"

I remembered my mother on the side porch, hitting the Indian on the head with the bristle end of a broom, saying, "Get away. No fire water, get away."

"Grampa," the little girl said, "pay attention!"

Nov. 2, 1984

Dear Ed.:

I would have written sooner, but Ettie had a major operation on her right foot Oct. 15 and since then has been plodding around with a ten-pound cast on that leg. So I have been elected to run the house, with considerable supervision. There have been the lighter moments, the neighbors autographing the plaster. One of the boys tried to put his signature on the good leg, which ended that sport.

I was very sad to find the enclosed notice in my mail. I have enjoyed both these publications and they have been an inspiration to me as an amateur entomologist. I hope the suspension was not because of any delinquency on my part in paying dues.

I presume you have not had time to sort out those three boxes of insects you took back to Ottawa with you, but I realized that there would be some numbered entries in my "diary" you would not have. Accordingly, I have photostated the record book up to date. It is also enclosed with this letter.

In the meantime I hope that both of you can pause long enough from your busy routines to have a most happy Christmas with your family.

And I will try to find some rare and unusual specimens for you in Florida.

Elwyn J. Farmer

"Is that a letter to Ed Becker?" Humphrey asked as he lifted me down into the greenhouse on the southeast side of the house. Henry sat in the other lawn chair reading the carbon copy of a letter to Ed Becker I wrote last winter. Sun poured in warm and dry. Outdoors and in the rest of the house the air was unseasonably chilly. But here my bones complained less of their everyday chores, standing, sitting, shifting. In a near field the house dog hurried along an invisible scent trail, head to the ground, tail wagging. The mist crept backward over the dunes, and patches of blue ocean showed through the mist. We were near the end of Cape Cod's graceful arm. Half a mile of field, marsh, and dunes, but no other homes, lay between this borrowed house and the Atlantic. My grandson Stephen was taking care of this home for part of the summer, and his father, brother, and I were freeloading for a week's time. The women had remained in Northampton because of the limited sleeping space here, and we were finding we could not cope. The excellent meals prepared by Humphrey and Henry, and our constant laughing, joking, and teasing, merely masked the desperate unhappiness of men without women.

I turned slightly to see if Humphrey had stayed behind me, but I heard noises in the kitchen that indicated he was pouring the coffee and turning the Canadian bacon one last time. When he returned, I said, "Yes."

"Yes what?" he asked. Then he remembered his original question and took the letter his father offered him. Humphrey cleared a space to sit beside Henry on the stone ledge, set his coffee between his thighs, and sighed. We had discovered the letter on the dining room table. It was probably "research" Stephen had liberated from my workbench in Montreal for the novel he was writing about me.

"Is Ed the entomologist at the Natural History Museum in Ottawa?" Henry asked.

Humphrey replied, "He's the one who's stealing our collection."

I laughed. "Our collection? You were a . . ." But the word would not come out. I saw it clearly spelled out in my mind, but a tissue-thin membrane prevented me from reaching and clearly comprehending it.

"What? A mercenary beetle collector?" Humphrey said, gently poking me in the ribs.

"That's close enough," I said.

"You call a penny a beetle payment?" my grandson said.

The mist over the dunes no longer had patches of blue shot through it, but patches of black, trembling like amoebas. Long ago I had concluded that these black spots in front of my eyes were my mind's way of resting, by limiting the details that came in. They were nothing to worry about.

"Why the period after Ed's name?" Henry asked. He showed me the "Ed." in question. "Because Ed is an abbreviation for Edward," I said.

"A nickname, Dad, not an abbreviation," said Henry, whose laughter always put me completely at ease.

• • •

Stephen emerged from the study yawning at the clatter of breakfast dishes being washed. "How did you sleep?" he asked me. "I put you in that bedroom downstairs here because you're too old and infirm to climb the front stairs, but also to test a hypothesis." Henry and Humphrey peered out from the kitchen. Stephen produced the dog, the reason he had been asked to take care of this house for part of the summer. "Let's see if she's grown any ticks since last night," Stephen said. The dog licked his hand while he gently straddled her. Then she realized what he was about to do. She whined and tried to shy away, but Stephen locked her between his knees. In the fold of skin under the front leg he found one tick, grown to the size of a cranberry. My grandson displayed a pair of tweezers like a surgeon, gripped the tick, and turned it counterclockwise. Stephen showed it around to prove that his system of dislodging the pest kept the head intact; then he dropped the tick into a large Mason jar of turpentine, where dozens of other bloated comrades had met a similar fate. Stephen pointed his tweezers at me. "Now you," he said. "That bed you slept in is reputed to be a haven for ticks."

"Oh yes," Humphrey said. "I'll hold his arms back."

Henry put a chair under the pine tree and the chair legs sank into the sandy earth as he climbed up. He raised his hands as if in prayer. "Like this?" he asked me.

"What do I know about bees?" I said, and the boys laughed.

"You're immune to their stings," Henry said. "Does that mean I am too?"

"Not immune," I said. "I just don't let them bother me."

"Now he tells me." Henry whistled a lullaby. Calmly, he laid a palm against the football-sized conglomeration of live bees that had attached themselves to the lowest branch. The bees had left their winter hibernation spot in an eave of the house the first warm day of summer. Bees cluster in the winter and swarm in the summer. They were not building a hive here, but the cold had returned and prevented the search for one elsewhere. The ball kept a constant temperature for the queen, who was in the middle. Workers constantly circulated, from the warm center to the cold exterior, then back to the middle again.

Humphrey still held me by the elbow. I could stand under my own power perfectly well now, but I enjoyed the pressure of his concern on my arm. Stephen stood ten feet away, screen door in hand. "Don't make them angry," he said. "I have to live with them for another month. You're only visiting."

"There," Henry said. "I'm touching them. It's a remarkably soft feeling. They begin to warm up at my touch and fan their wings. You're right, Dad; they seem to be moving all the time, like a dance marathon. Where are my glasses, Humphrey?" His son reached into the tall grass at our feet and miraculously pulled reading glasses out. "Thanks," Henry said. "Ah, I can see the drowsy ones on the outside being tapped on the shoulders by the warm ones from inside. There's something obscene about watching this.

"El," he said, stepping down from the chair to let Humphrey have a crack at the bees, "do you remember when we first moved to Minneapolis? You took me downtown and said, 'Henry, you've got to see the most remarkable thing.' We pulled up in front of a woman's lingerie store at night. The windows were full of headless manikins wearing bras and girdles. The shape of the windows and the bright lights the store kept on all night attracted all sorts of insects. You stood there an hour, with an aspirator tube at your lips, for all the world looking like a pervert studying every sacred inch of those undergarments."

"Who said I wasn't," I said.

"For all their dominance over the earth insects are afraid of water," I said. Humphrey grunted. He was on the narrow sandbank of this lake. He had trapped a tiger beetle with his net and was in the middle of the delicate operation of transferring it to the killing bottle. "What?" he said, not looking up. Hard reeds behind him clacked in the breeze. I could count four ticks clinging to his white silk shirt. The shirt was part of his waiter's uniform in New York City. He had given up collecting ten years ago, but he picked up the old skills with astonishing recall. He would never live what my generation considered a proper Christian life, being a homosexual, a waiter, and a New Yorker (I've never overcome my dislike of that city), but my wife and I love and favor him as much as we ever have, which Stephen seems to accept with more and more grace.

Stephen said, "What about water beetles, or those spiders that trap air in their web and live for hours under water? I saw them on TV." Stephen sat in a low beach chair, *Boston Globe* flapping so that he could not read it for more than a few seconds in a row without cursing and straightening it out.

"None of those breathe under water," I said. "Only a handful of species are truly aquatic."

"As opposed to semiaquatic," Humphrey said. He was always listening, even when he didn't appear to be. "Like the water strider, or that spider you saw, Stephen."

Another heavy truck lumbered over the road a dozen yards behind us. Stephen had shown us the illegal addition to a house being built down the road from his house. The homes on this hill had been allowed to stand and the original owners to inhabit them for the remainder of their lifetimes after the 1961 legislation that made this land part of the National Seashore. This truck was carrying more cement or materials to that site. The engine slowed. Another smaller engine came into range of our hearing. The two engine sounds meshed for a moment; then the smaller one became distinct again as the car motored to the highway a few hundred yards away. The truck seemed to stay in place, but there was little room and no reason for it to stop on the deserted stretch of road through this marshland.

"What's he doing?" Stephen asked. "He's not moving." We heard the driver talking, then swearing. Then the engine dieseled and died. The driver swore again; then all was silent until we heard the sound of sneakers landing on pavement and sneakers running off. "The truck broke down," Stephen said. "He's going to get help. Serves him right." Stephen stood up to look through the bulrushes. "Let's go sabotage the truck."

I had found a comfortable position, on my side, sifting dry, tangled beach grass for insect life. This was the only position that did not send sharp stabs of pain into the cancerous bone of my right hip.

"You be our scout," Humphrey said.

"Oh to be young, handsome, and agile," I said.

Stephen darted into the reeds. A few moments later he convinced us to "come and see." The truck had apparently pulled onto the shoulder of the road to let the car pass, but it was an unreliable shoulder. The soft earth quickly gave way and the truck had tipped over on its side, half of it sinking into peat that was still burping when we arrived.

I woke up to the overwhelming urge for red licorice. Half-burned curtains greeted me when I put my glasses on. Out the window stretched endless marshland and low ridges of scrub pine. I dressed quickly and went downstairs. At the desk I discovered I was in Flin Flon, Manitoba, the Prince Edward Hotel. The fellow behind the desk asked, "What's your business?" "Give me another hour and I'll remember," I said. He laughed and I asked him directions to the nearest candy store. I left the hotel by the back way, as instructed, and stumbled over a man who lay on the boardwalk. The sun streaming down Division Street blinded me. "Excuse me," I said, groping for a wall. But a terrible smell entered my blindness. Flies swarmed up at me from below. The man groaned, "Not again. You've already done your job." When I could see, I saw a soot-faced miner sprawled on his back. His overalls glistened darkly at the belly, and the slats of white pine underneath him were red. A hunter's knife jutted from his hip. I blinked and looked again. My first thought was: How can a blade have penetrated that bone? A flash of light caught my eye: sun glinting off the belt buckle of the bank manager on the far side of the street. Plenty of townspeople must already have witnessed this scene. I cried out to the half dozen within my sight, "Won't someone call a doctor?" The crowd reacted like startled rats, scurrying off in all directions. Then I felt a stab in my own hip, sympathetic pain. "I'll get help," I said.

"Mind your own business, bug collector," the wounded man growled.

Henry and I were on the path back to the house. The day had grown hot. We disturbed a pair of bobwhites, who raced ahead of us a few yards, then sensed what poor predators we were, and slowed to our pace. I told Henry I'd had a dream about the stabbing victim I stumbled over in Peace River. "Except it was Flin Flon in the dream," I said. "I have no idea why."

"Maybe because the terrain in Flin Flon is similar to this."

"You're right," I said, amazed by this insight.

"Say," Henry said, "you can tell that story to Stephen. I'm sure he could use it."

But just then we heard the boys' voices. Our path ran alongside the yard north of the house. Stephen and Humphrey seemed to be sitting at the picnic table, drinks with clinking ice cubes in their hands.

"I dunno," Stephen said. "I can't believe he would do it."

"Nonsense," Humphrey said, dismissing his brother's thought out of hand, as he always did. "If it gets too bad you know he has the resources. He could kill the whole town of Roxboro with all that potassium cyanide in the basement."

Henry's arm flew out and I bumped into his palm. My son turned and crashed through the brush. "Boys," he shouted. "I left Grampa collecting in the dunes on his side for a few minutes and when I returned he was fast asleep on a nice little bed of sand. You should have seen it. Grampa has a great story for you, Stephen."

"Is Grampa with you now?" Stephen said, alarmed.

"Listen," Humphrey said. I pulled back brambles and stepped quietly through to the other side, joining my offspring at the picnic table. They were all looking toward the house, where the ball of bees had begun to swarm. It sounded like an old but very reliable machine going full tilt. "It's beautiful," Humphrey said, and he turned to me with tears in his eyes. "They don't sting when they swarm, do they?"

"No," I said. "It's a sexual frenzy. They've got other things on their minds."

"Let's go see," Humphrey said.

Only a thin tongue of wax hung from the branch that once held the ball of bees. The air was full of insects in ecstasy. They bombarded us, but our smell did not trigger any alarms. Somewhere in the swarm the queen gave off a powerful pheromone that said, "Break camp, children. A permanent home has been found."